After All

Also by Kristen Proby

The Romancing Manhattan Series
All the Way • All It Takes • After All

The Fusion Series
Listen to Me • Close to You • Blush for Me
The Beauty of Us • Savor You

The Boudreaux Series
Easy Love • Easy with You • Easy Charm
Easy Melody • Easy for Keeps • Easy Kisses
Easy Magic • Easy Nights

With Me in Seattle Series
Come Away With Me • Under the Mistletoe With Me
Fight With Me • Play With Me • Rock With Me
Safe With Me • Tied With Me • Breathe With Me
Forever With Me • Stay With Me • Love With Me
Dance With Me • Wonder With Me
Dream With Me • You Belong With Me

Love Under the Big Sky Series
Loving Cara • Seducing Lauren
Falling for Jillian • Saving Grace
Charming Hannah • Kissing Jenna
Waiting for Willa • Tempting Brooke
Soaring With Fallon
Enchanting Sebastian
Enticing Liam

After All

A Romancing Manhattan Novel

KRISTEN
PROBY

AVON

An Imprint of HarperCollinsPublishers

AFTER ALL. Copyright © 2020 by Kristen Proby. All rights reserved.
Printed in the United States of America. No part of this book may be
used or reproduced in any manner whatsoever without written permission
except in the case of brief quotations embodied in critical articles and re-
views. For information, address HarperCollins Publishers, 195 Broadway,
New York, NY 10007.

HarperCollins books may be purchased for educational, business, or sales
promotional use. For information, please email the Special Markets De-
partment at SPsales@harpercollins.com.

FIRST EDITION

Designed by Diahann Sturge

Library of Congress Cataloging-in-Publication Data has been applied for.

ISBN 978-0-06-289268-3

20 21 22 23 24   LSC   10 9 8 7 6 5 4 3 2 1

After All

Prologue

~Nora~

I'm not Mrs. Shaw."

The receptionist frowns up at me. She's new.

"I'm on the approved list to pick Gabby up from school, if her father is unavailable," I elaborate and wait while the woman before me taps on her keyboard, then nods her head.

"Here you are. Okay then, Gabby is in Mrs. Flynn's office. You're free to go on in."

"Thanks." My heels click on the floor as I march into the principal's office. Gabby's dark head is bowed, and Mrs. Flynn's hands are folded on her desk, waiting patiently for me.

"Hello, Nora," she says politely. "Thank you for coming."

"You're welcome. Carter's been in court all afternoon. I'm sorry you couldn't reach him."

"Dad's always in court," Gabby mutters.

"What's this all about?"

Mrs. Flynn looks over to Gabby. "Would you like to explain it to her?"

"Not really."

I sigh. Since Gabby's reached the preteen years, she's been more and more difficult.

"What's up, Gabby?"

My boss's daughter shrugs one shoulder. "I was sticking up for my friend. That's all."

I blink at Mrs. Flynn and raise an eyebrow. "I suspect that's not all."

"Another student, Claire, claims Gabby assaulted her and pulled her earring out of her ear."

"Gabby!"

"She's mean," Gabby insists. "Like, really mean. And I was sick and tired of listening to her bully Lily."

"Our school has a zero tolerance policy when it comes to these things," Mrs. Flynn says patiently. "I'll be speaking with Claire, the girl whose ear is now bandaged up, but Gabby, you're suspended until Monday."

"What?" Gabby demands. "But it's only Thursday."

"That's the policy," Mrs. Flynn says. "I'll make an appointment to speak with your father about this further."

"Let's go," I say as Gabby stands and reaches for her bookbag. To the principal I say, "Thanks for everything."

The principal nods as Gabby and I leave her office and I immediately reach for my phone and dial Carter's number. It goes to voice mail, and I leave the second message since I received the call from the school.

"Me again. I have Gabby. Will tell you more when I see you, but she's not hurt."

I hang up and Gabby and I climb into the waiting taxi. She's scowling as she puts her seat belt on.

"This freaking sucks."

"Totally," I agree as we pull away from the school. "Want to tell me about it?"

"No. I'll have to tell Dad everything anyway. I'd rather only tell the story once."

"Okay." This surprises her. She whips her head around to stare at me with wide eyes. "I think you've had a rough day."

"Yeah." Her voice cracks.

"You know you have to give me your phone."

She silently pulls the device from her pocket and passes it to me.

"But I think you might need an ice cream."

"I can have ice cream for being suspended?"

"No. You can have ice cream because you've had a rough day. It's not my job to punish you, aside from retrieving your phone. The rest is up to your dad and the school. Also, I could use some ice cream myself."

And maybe some vodka, but that's not possible right now.

On our way to the office, I have the cab drop us at our favorite ice cream shop and we leave with two scoops each.

"So you were sticking up for your friend?" I ask as we walk

into the office building where I work for Gabby's dad. The ice cream shop is just down the block.

"Yeah."

"Did you have to make the other girl bleed?"

"I didn't mean to," she admits. "It just sort of . . . happened."

"Well, you'll have to tell me the story sometime."

She nods as we walk to the elevator.

"I'm in so much trouble," Gabby mutters, staring at her strawberry ice cream.

"Maybe not. I'll talk to your dad before I send him into the office."

"You're the best," she says with a grin. "What would I do without you?"

"We'll never have to know," I assure her as we reach our floor. Gabby beelines it into her dad's office, and I call him one last time to leave a message that we're back at his office.

This is a pretty typical day in the life for me as Carter Shaw's assistant. I don't just work as his legal assistant, although that is technically my job title. No, for five years I've helped with *everything*, from picking Gabby up from school to hiring and firing housekeepers and nannies. I work fourteen-hour days. I am married to the job.

But I wouldn't have it any other way.

"The preteen drama queen is in your office," I inform Carter when he comes walking into the office with his brother-in-law Quinn. "She's been suspended until Monday, and I already have her phone in my desk. But Carter."

He stops and looks down at me with worried blue eyes. I can see that he's impatient to get to his daughter, to find out what the hell is going on.

"You really need to listen to her before you fly off the handle."

"I don't fly off the handle," Carter replies. I roll my eyes.

"Of course. You're completely calm at all times."

"Thanks for taking care of things, Nora," Carter says as he walks to his door and both men walk into the office.

Every day is the same.

Thanks for taking care of things, Nora.

About thirty minutes later, the three of them come walking back out of the office. Quinn hugs Gabby, nods at me, and heads to his office.

"We're headed home," Carter says grimly. Gabby's still looking miserable, but no longer scared, and that makes me happy. Her father may have moments of impatience, but he's right, he's rarely flown off the handle. I just know that when she tells him she made Claire bleed, his temper may flare.

"Do you want me to drop dinner by later?"

"Oh, I'm full," Gabby says. "That ice cream filled me up."

Carter stops and stares down at his daughter, then over to me. "You rewarded her for being suspended by *taking her for ice cream*?"

"I didn't reward her, or punish her, for anything."

"Christ," he mutters. "You need to remember your place, Nora. Taking my daughter out for ice cream after picking her up from school is not that place."

I'm shell-shocked. *Are you fucking kidding me?*

But before I can respond, Carter grabs Gabby's hand and they disappear down the hallway to the elevator.

I need to remember my place.

I DIDN'T SLEEP well last night. I tossed and turned, Carter's voice in my head, until I finally flung the covers off and started cleaning my apartment.

It sparkles this morning, and I'm no less pissed off.

I'm in the employee lounge, pouring my second cup of coffee of the day, when Carter comes walking in the room.

"Leave us," he says, effectively clearing the room. His voice is hard, his hands shoved in his pockets.

The last person out of the room shuts the door behind them. I don't pause as I stir the sugar and cream in my coffee, watching him with cool eyes.

I'm damn pissed.

"Nora," he begins, and then he sighs. "We need to talk."

"You bet your ass we need to talk," I reply, setting my cup aside and walking to him, seeing red. All my frustration and anger has bubbled up, and there's no stopping it now. "You're my boss, and I respect you, but you do *not* get to talk to me like that. I need to know my *place*, Carter? Well, for the past five years, my *place* has been doing whatever the hell you need me to do for you, including parent your child. I take her on the weekends you work. I take her to the doctor. I take her to after-school activities."

I shove my finger in his chest, on a roll.

"Don't you—"

"Would you stop running your damn mouth for two seconds?" He grabs my wrist and pulls me against his tall, lean body. He's breathing hard, his blue eyes are bright. "I'm trying to apologize here. So if you'd stop dressing me down for a minute, I could get the words out."

"Go on." I swallow hard, trying to ignore the fact that this is more physical contact than I've ever had with Carter in my life. He's warm and firm, and I'm not proud of the way my breath hitches when he leans his face closer to mine.

"I'm sorry for what I said." His voice is calmer now. "I was out of line. I was upset at Gabby, and I took it out on you. You didn't deserve that."

His eyes fall to my lips and his breath catches. Is that lust I see in his eyes?

"I don't know what we'd do without you, Nora. I'm sorry for what I said."

"Okay."

"Do you forgive me?"

I swallow hard and nod. "Yeah. Of course."

I can't think straight. I need to pull away. To escape back to the safety of my desk. But we don't pull away. Instead, Carter leans farther into me, as if he's unable to fight it. His hand slides from my hip, up to my ribs, and my nipples tighten, yearning for his touch. I don't have time to question our actions as his mouth descends toward me, but just before his lips land on mine, the door opens, and we spring apart, staring at each other in shock.

"Oh, sorry," Stephanie from payroll says. "I didn't know anyone was in here. I can come back—"

"Don't be silly," Carter says, his intense gaze still pinned to mine. "We were just leaving."

He turns and marches out of the room, leaving me shell-shocked again.

"Nora? You okay?"

I smile at Stephanie and nod. "Of course. Still waking up. Didn't sleep well."

I retrieve my coffee and leave the lounge, headed for my desk.

What in the ever-loving hell just happened?

Chapter One

~Nora~

*H*ey, thanks for taking care of things today, Nora."

I glance up from one of my three computer monitors to see Carter standing by my desk, smiling down at me. A dimple winks in his left cheek, sending a flash of warmth down my spine.

In the four months since I brought Gabby back to the office from school for maiming her bratty little classmate, I've felt a shift where Carter's concerned. It's purely one-sided. I'm positive of it.

Since that day in the lounge, since the almost-kiss, I've noticed that Carter's hot as hell.

He's remained perfectly professional and normal, as if nothing happened at all. I've worked closely with the man for almost ten years. I know him. And nothing has indicated that he's interested in anything other than my ability to basically make his life run smoothly.

Which is absolutely how it *should* be.

But damn it, my hormones have suddenly kicked in.

It's ridiculous.

Just like that dimple in his left cheek is ridiculous.

"Nora?"

"What? Oh." I shake myself out of my weird haze of lust and blink. "Sorry. Been a long day."

"You've been here longer than I have, and I'm running on thirteen hours," he replies, checking his watch. "I think we should both knock off for the day."

"Is it that late?" I check the time on the corner of my monitor and sigh. "Wow. I just have a few more—"

"It'll wait until tomorrow," he interrupts. "Shut it down, Nora. I'll wait for you."

"Wait for me to what?"

He quirks a brow. "To walk you to your car."

"Oh. All right."

Carter nods, then walks back to his office and I sigh deeply. For the love of the baby Jesus in a manger, what in the hell is wrong with me? This is Carter Shaw, my boss, the man I've worked with for most of my adult life, and I'm suddenly nervous around him? It's stupid.

And it's going to stop *today*.

I make quick work of shutting down the computer, locking up my notes and the physical planner that I keep on hand. Everything is in the shared drive, of course, but I have hard copies of everything, in case the power goes out or there's a zombie apocalypse.

Prepared is an understatement for what I am.

Once I've gathered my handbag and jacket from the closet behind me, which is hidden in the wall and reminds me of a secret passageway, Carter emerges from his office, locks his door behind him, and turns to me with that smile again.

But I'm immune.

I'm immune, I remind myself.

"Ready?" he asks.

"Sure." We walk in silence to the elevator. I glance to the left and see a light coming from Finn's office. This law firm is owned by Carter and his two brothers-in-law, Quinn and Finn Cavanaugh. "Is Finn working late?"

"Yeah, the Barkowski case is driving him crazy."

"Going on three months now," I reply as the elevator doors open. "You have a meeting with them tomorrow afternoon."

Carter just nods and watches me for a long moment as we begin our descent to the garage under the building. Most buildings in Manhattan don't have parking garages. But this is a newer structure, and the Cavanaugh/Shaw brothers wanted fancy.

Fancy is what they got.

"What?" I ask with a frown when he continues to watch me.

"You always know literally everything that's happening in this building."

"Of course I do."

"How do you do that?"

I smirk. "I listen. I watch. It's a matter of paying attention."

"My mom always used to say she had eyes in the back of her head," he replies with a laugh, shoving one hand in his pocket.

"You could call it that," I concede with a smile. "I have to know what's going on so I can be one step ahead of you. Your schedule, what you may need. That's my job."

"And you're damn good at it," he murmurs. The comment fills me with pride. Who doesn't want their boss to say that their work is noticed and appreciated?

"Thanks." The doors open and we walk into the cold. "Jesus, this winter is going to suck."

"It already does," he agrees, pulling the collar of his coat up around his neck. Rather than hurrying over to his own Mercedes, he walks with me to my car and waits as I open the door.

"You didn't have to walk me to my car," I say as I look up at him and freeze when he brushes a piece of my hair behind my ear. Just that simple touch has me forgetting all about the bitter winter cold.

He doesn't reply. His blue eyes watch his fingers as they brush down my neck, and then he backs up a step and shoves both hands in his pockets.

"Drive safe," he says with a nod, then hurries over to his vehicle.

I watch as he starts his car but he doesn't pull away. After a moment, he rolls down his window. "Aren't you going to get in?"

"Oh. Right. Have a good night." I numbly start my own car and follow Carter out of the garage, then turn the opposite way as him and drive home. I live in a small apartment in Manhattan. Close to work *and* to Carter, should he ever need anything.

Which I know sounds a little too dedicated, but he pays me well, and I don't mind.

Not many personal assistants in this city bring in a salary generous enough to pay for twelve hundred square feet in Manhattan, with a parking garage where they work, full insurance benefits, and a nice retirement plan. I don't have to take public transportation.

I'm spoiled.

So you bet your ass I'm dedicated to Carter.

Did it hurt my marriage? Yes, but many things led to the demise of that relationship, not just a demanding career. It didn't help that my ex was threatened by the fact that I *am* successful. It wouldn't matter who I worked for.

But that's in the past, and I'm happy with my life.

Someone's parked in my designated parking spot, again, so I circle until I find a space, then shoot a quick text off to my super, informing him that someone needs to be towed, and hurry inside where it's warm.

To top it off, the elevator is broken. Also again. So I slug it up the four flights to my floor and breathe heavily as I toss my handbag and briefcase on my kitchen counter. I've just opened the fridge to reach for my bottle of water when the front door bursts open and my best friend, Christopher, makes a dramatic entrance.

"This place is a dump," he announces as he drops onto a stool at the breakfast bar.

"Hello to you, too." I drink my water and watch him, amused. Our building is anything *but* a dump. It's actually really nice. But Christopher isn't patient when it comes to things breaking down.

"The elevator isn't working again," he says. "I had to take the stairs down here, which means I'll have to take them back up again."

I drink my water, eyeing his six-foot frame. "You're a freaking dancer. You're in shape. Two flights of stairs are a breeze for you."

"That's not the point." He sets a brown bag on the counter and my stomach growls. "You're hungry, darling."

"Starving. What did you bring me?"

"Pastrami on rye," he says as he pulls the sandwich out of the bag and passes it to me. "Your favorite."

"God bless you." I unwrap the wax paper and sink my teeth into the still-warm goodness. "Smph gmph."

"You're such a lady," he says with a laugh.

"I know." I swallow the bite of goodness and take a swig of water. "Where's yours?"

"I already ate it. You've been working late a lot lately."

"Work's busy. It's not a big deal."

"You have bags under your eyes. But you're in luck because I brought eye patches." He pulls the patches out of his back pocket. "And they're still cold from the freezer. Come here, I'll put them on for you."

"You come to me, I'm eating."

"Such a diva," he says as he circles the island and opens the pouches, then arranges the cold tabs under my eyes. They're strangely soothing. "There, these will get rid of the bags. And the dark circles."

"I think you just told me I look like shit."

"That's not at all what I said." He kisses my cheek then returns to his stool. "You're always beautiful. But you work too hard, and your eyes are tired."

"What would I do without you here to take care of me?"

"I shudder to think about it." He shivers dramatically, because just about everything he does in life is dramatic, and makes me laugh.

"How's Alonzo?" I ask before taking another bite of my pastrami.

"Who?" He frowns.

"The dude you were dating two weeks ago."

"Oh. Right. I have no idea."

I raise a brow. "What happened?"

"He's an idiot. Took one and a half dates to figure it out."

"Faster than the last one." I shrug and polish off the sandwich, then sigh in happiness. "Should I be this in love with a sandwich?"

"It's a pretty good sandwich," he says. "What else is going on with you?"

"What do you mean?"

Christopher rolls his eyes. "I'm your best friend, Nora. Something's been up with you, I just haven't been able to put my finger on it. If I didn't know better, I'd say you were having man issues, but we got rid of that issue last year."

I sigh and toss my garbage in the recycle bin and then lead him to the living room where we sit on my incredibly comfortable couch. "Okay, I'm just going to be blunt."

"That's the way we do things, honey."

"Why do I suddenly think Carter's hot?"

"Uh, because he *is* hot. Duh." Christopher tilts his head. "Please don't tell me you're just now figuring that out. I mean, I understand that you were married, but you weren't dead."

"I've always known he's handsome, but he's my boss, and up until a year ago, I *was* married."

"To an idiot, and like I said, not dead," he says, but I ignore him. I stand and pace the living room.

"But lately, I've noticed things. Like the dimple in his left cheek, and the way his ass looks in slacks. And he's started turning that charming smile that he usually aims at clients on me, and I'm not sure what to make of it."

"Sounds like your hormones are recovering from the divorce. And for the record, it's about damn time."

"But *not* with my boss," I reply, shaking my head fiercely. "This can't happen. I can't have an affair with Carter. I love my job, and I have opportunities there. I'm not going to throw it all away because Carter has a nice ass. I'm not an idiot."

"You're definitely *not* an idiot," he agrees. "And workplace romances are typically disastrous. Remember me and Stephan?"

"Who?"

"It doesn't matter. You're right. It can only end badly. So stop looking at his ass and focus on work. We'll find you a suitable man somewhere else."

"Why do you sound like my grandmother?"

Christopher laughs. "I'm way cooler than your grandmother."

"Besides, I'm being a little presumptuous. Just because I think Carter's hot doesn't mean he feels the same way. In fact, I'm sure he doesn't. He's always perfectly professional."

Except when he almost kisses me in the employee lounge and walks me to my car and tucks my hair behind my ear. But I don't tell Christopher that part.

"You're totally right. You're beautiful, and he's blind as a friggin' bat if he doesn't see it. I'm telling you, I think you're ready to get back out there, and that's great news. So now you just have to redirect that energy to dating."

"Gross." I stick my tongue out and gag. "I don't want to date. I don't know *how* to date. It just seems like too much energy."

"Well, where are you going to put this sexual tension if you don't date, Nora? Besides, you're too pretty and too much fun to die alone."

"Thanks, I think."

"You could date online."

"I would literally rather pluck every hair from my body than online date."

Christopher nods in agreement. "You just need to get out more. Go to the gym. The grocery. Central Park."

"I'm not looking for a serial killer."

"Honey, they all frequent the same places. It's a crapshoot."

"Awesome."

IT'S BEEN FIVE days since Carter walked me to my car after work. Three workdays and a weekend. I spent Saturday with Gabby, shopping for new throw pillows for my apartment, and I think I can safely say that I've shaken off the weirdness from the past few months.

It was just hormones, that's all. I mean, I am *not* interested in Carter. I know him too well. I *work* for him.

The thought of it is just silly.

"Good morning." Carter sets a Starbucks mug on my desk and I look up in confusion.

"Good morning. You brought me coffee?"

"Sure. I stopped and got me some, so I grabbed you one, too. Well, a chai because that's your favorite. Oh, and a muffin."

He pulls the muffin, in a small paper bag, out of his pocket and sets it next to my tea.

"Thanks."

"You're welcome." He winks, that dimple making an appearance in his cheek again, and turns to his office. But before he disappears inside, he turns back to me. "Do you need anything?"

"Wait a minute, that's *my* line. Do you have a fever? Do you need me to make an appointment with Dr. Hansen?"

But Carter just laughs and disappears into his office, leaving me with a chai, a muffin, and complete confusion.

Since when does he fetch *me* coffee? And ask if I need anything?

He must be sick.

I check his appointments and see he's scheduled for his annual checkup in two weeks. Maybe I should move it up.

"Hey, Nora," Quinn says as he walks past my desk. "How's it going?"

"I can't complain," I reply. "Is he expecting you?"

"Yep, he called me in," Quinn replies.

"Would you like anything? Coffee? Breakfast?"

Quinn stops next to my desk and smiles kindly. His new wedding ring shines on his left hand.

"How's Sienna?" I ask. I like Quinn's new wife. She's kind, and an excellent attorney.

"She's amazing. And moving into her new office today."

"Awesome. Good for her. I'll go see if she needs anything."

"You'd better watch yourself, Nora. I might just try to steal you away from Carter."

I smile. All three of the partners are handsome, funny, and kind men. Working for any of them would be great.

"I'm afraid I'm stuck with Carter. I know too much. He'd have to kill me before he'd let me quit."

"You're probably right," Quinn replies with a nod. "Have a good day, Nora."

"You, too."

With Carter busy, I hurry down the hall to Sienna's new office and knock on the doorframe.

"Hey," she says with a smile when she sees me. "Come on in."

"I just saw Quinn and he said you were here, so I thought I'd check on you. Do you need anything?"

"A stiff drink would be great," she says with a laugh. Sienna has amazing red hair that's currently pulled into a tasteful knot. "I'm really fine. We've been talking about me coming to work here for months, so I shouldn't be nervous."

"Starting a new job is always nerve-racking. Have you hired an assistant yet?"

"It's on the list for this month."

"Would you like me to weed through the résumés and schedule interviews for you?"

She stares at me for a full fifteen seconds before answering. "Holy cow, Nora, are you serious?"

"Of course, I'm happy to help. We'll ease you in. And in the meantime, just let me know if you need anything."

"You already have a full workload—"

"It's fine," I insist. "And temporary. I'm happy to help."

"I owe you lunch."

"I'll collect." I smile and turn to leave.

"Oh, Nora?"

"Yeah?"

"I know where everything is, and I think I have all the supplies I need, but I could use help figuring out the online scheduling."

"No problem. I'll stop by this afternoon while Carter's in a meeting."

"Thanks."

I walk back to my own desk, nodding at colleagues as I make my way down the hall. In the employee break room, I hear two female voices, which isn't out of the ordinary, but when I hear my name, I stop and listen.

"I mean, Nora's been here *forever*. And I'm sure she's great at her job, but you'll never convince me that Carter's kept her around this long for her scheduling skills. You *know* they're fucking when no one else is around."

"I don't know, they never give off that vibe." That's Stephanie from payroll. The other voice is Mary from HR. Both have only been here for about a year.

"Well, of course not. There's a no-frat policy here," Mary continues. "But she literally handles everything for him. She even picks Gabby up from school sometimes."

"She's his assistant," Stephanie says. "And honestly, I don't think it's any of our business."

"If you two have time to stand in here and gossip about your coworkers, you don't have enough work to do," I say from the doorway, making them both jump and flush with embarrassment. "And if you have a problem with me, you can come to *me* to voice it."

"No problem," Mary says immediately and swallows hard. "I was just going back to my desk."

She slips past me and hurries down the hall, and I turn to Stephanie and raise my eyebrows.

"She has a crush on Carter," Stephanie says with a sigh. "And she's catty about it."

"That's a nice way to put it."

"I'm going back to work, too. I should have known better than to come down for a third cup of coffee. I don't need that much caffeine."

"Pour a fresh cup. Something tells me you need it."

She shrugs. "I hate office gossip."

"Me, too."

Chapter Two

~Carter~

"Do you have a fever?" I mutter and rest my forehead on the closed door of my office. "Smooth, Carter. Real fucking smooth. I've clearly lost the charm I'm known for in the courtroom."

I walk to my desk and fall into the chair, rubbing my lips in agitation. What the fuck is wrong with me? Why is this so hard?

I've always known that Nora's great. I would be crippled without her here at the office. She's an extension of me here, and usually knows what I need before I do.

But four months ago, after the encounter in the lounge where I almost kissed the hell out of her, my feelings toward her have changed.

Or, if I'm being honest, my eyes have opened.

She's not just a fantastic assistant.

She's a fascinating woman. Intelligent, funny, and so damn

beautiful it's hard to look at her. My fingers itch to plunge into her thick, blond hair. Her body, with luscious curves in all the right damn places, is a siren's call, and with each day that passes, I'm finding it harder and harder to stay away.

Only two other people know how I feel. My best friends in the world, Quinn and Finn.

Finn's out of the office today, so I pick up the phone and dial Quinn's number.

"Yo," he says, distracted.

"Come to my office, please."

"On my way."

We hang up and I stand to pace my office. The space is three times as big as my first apartment, and none of the furniture came from IKEA. No, we had an expensive firm come in and do the place up right.

I was afraid to sit on the leather couch situated in front of the fireplace for three months when I first moved in.

"What's up?" Quinn asks as he saunters into my space and flops on the couch, one leg propped on the other. "Issues with the Sanduski case?"

"No, the Nora case," I mutter and shove my hands in my pockets, the way I always do when I'm agitated.

"Did you finally ask her out?"

"No."

"Carter, none of us are getting any younger," Quinn says with a heavy sigh. "For the love of God, just ask the woman out to dinner."

"There are several reasons that this is a bad idea," I remind him and sit across from him, holding up a finger. "One, she's my employee. Not only that, she's been with me for almost ten years now. She's been through pretty much every aspect of my career in New York. The death of Darcy. *Everything.* If I screw this up, we don't just go our separate ways and chalk it up to dating experience."

"Great, you don't have to explain your baggage to her. She's already up to speed."

"Two," I continue without acknowledging his comment. "We have a no-fraternization policy in our firm. It's not ethical, and completely cliché, to start a relationship with my secretary. She could sue us."

"I don't think she'll sue us, unless you ask her out for dinner and it doesn't go well. Besides, I won't tell if you don't." Quinn's lips tip up in a smirk. "I met *my* wife at work. Hell, for workaholics like us, this is the only place to meet people. Unless you want to try online dating."

"No. Absolutely not."

"Well, then, this is your only option."

"How in the hell do you flirt?" I ask bluntly.

Quinn stares at me for a long moment and then replies with "Do you have a fever?"

"Jesus." I rub my hands briskly over my face. "No, I don't have a fever. I've been out of this game for a *long* time, Quinn. I met your sister in college, for God's sake. It was easier in college."

"Are you calling my sister *easy?*"

I glance over at him. He's smiling at his own joke.

"Is this weird?"

"Yes, you should have asked her out months ago."

"Not that. *This*. You're giving me dating advice and I was married to your sister. How are you and Finn so cool with this?"

"I love my sister," Quinn begins, his face sobering. "And I miss her every damn day. If she were alive, and you were talking like this, I'd kick your ass all the way to Miami and back, but she isn't, Carter. She's been gone for *five years*. It's okay for you to move on and be happy."

"I know," I say softly. "But I just want to make sure *you* know because my life is forever tied to your family. Not just because of Gabby, but also because of our business and the fact that you're *my* family. So I need you all to be cool with me dating someone new."

"You're not a monk," Quinn replies easily. "You've grieved long enough. Find a girl who makes you happy. And if that's Nora, I say go for it. We own the damn company. We can change the no-frat policy if we need to."

"She might say no."

"She might say yes. So just *ask her*."

"Okay. You're right."

"Of course I am."

"Thanks for coming over so I could talk it out."

"No problem. Oh, don't forget, that blizzard's coming in later today. You'll want to get out of here early."

"What in the hell is up with the weather this year?" I grumble. "We never get this much snow."

"Well, we do, just not often. It's supposed to dump tonight. I'm leaving soon to go check on Mom."

"Tell her I say hi."

"Will do."

Quinn shuts the door behind him and I turn to the windows, looking out on a white New York.

"Carter?"

I turn to find Nora in my doorway. Her hair is down today, golden around her shoulders. She's in one of her power suits, red today. And as always, she's in heels.

Let's not even discuss how many times I've imagined those heels propped on my shoulders.

I'm losing my mind.

"Your nine o'clock is here."

"Thanks." I nod. "Send them in."

She smiles and turns away, speaking to my client.

Flirting with Nora will have to wait for later.

"Hello."

"Happy birthday, Mom." I immediately begin rubbing my forehead. I hate this annual phone call and waited until the end of the day to make it.

"Thank you. How are things with you, Carter?"

"Things are going well. New York is under a bit of snow right now."

"Well, if you were in Georgia where you belong, you wouldn't have the snow problem, would you?"

And there it is. Not even five sentences into a call and she starts laying on the guilt trip.

"How are you and Dad?"

"As well as can be expected, of course," she says with a dramatic sigh. "Your father is still working long days at the hospital. I stay busy with charity work and my volunteering opportunities."

I wonder how many men she's slept with this year that constitutes her *volunteering opportunities*.

"I'm glad to hear you're both staying busy."

"Your father should be retiring now."

"He certainly *can* retire, Mom. He's earned it."

"You know that's not possible. If you'd gone into medicine like you should have, and taken over his business, he would have been able to retire."

"So he's just going to work until the day he dies out of spite? Because I didn't want to be a doctor and take over the family business?"

"It's been in his family for five generations. I can't believe I raised such a stubborn, selfish son."

"Me neither," I reply quietly. "Gabby's doing well. Not that you asked."

"Just move home," she says with a sigh. "Pack you and Gabby up and move here, where you belong. You've grieved *that woman* long enough, Carter. You should be here with your family. I'm quite certain you can work as an attorney here. Someone's always suing someone else."

"We *are* with our family." The headache is pulsing in my forehead now. "And *that woman* was my wife."

"Oh, I'm well aware. I sat through that horrible wedding and held my tongue."

"You did not hold your tongue."

No, my mother stood up in front of two hundred people and announced that she didn't support my marrying a poor woman from New York, and that I was making the biggest mistake of my life.

"Certain things were expected of you."

"I'm sorry I was an only child," I reply firmly. "I feel bad for you and Dad, that you didn't have a child who wanted to live the life *you* wanted them to. But I'm forty years old, Mother, and I think it's time for you to come to terms with the fact that I'm living the life I want to. The life I've worked hard for."

"I will *not* have you speak badly of my dead wife when she's not here to defend herself against you."

"Well, I always say, what goes around comes around, and she—"

"If you say Darcy died because of karma, I will never speak to you again and make sure you never see Gabby, either."

"I don't see her anyway." Her voice begins to tremble now, marking the manipulation portion of our program. "I don't ever see my only grandchild. You've stripped us of the opportunity to know her at all."

"No, I haven't."

"I don't know why you call. If you want to upset me on my birthday, you achieve that goal every year."

"I call because it's your birthday, and because I'll always wish things were different. But this will be my last phone call, Mother."

She hangs up without saying good-bye, and I sigh deeply. I press the heels of my hands into my eyes.

Of course I'm not going to expose my daughter to *that*. Why on earth would I?

When I glance up, I notice it's dark outside, and I frown.

How did the day slip away from me?

Is Nora still here?

I open my office door, and sure enough, there she is, typing away on her keyboard.

"Why didn't you go home?" I ask.

She frowns up at me. "Because I have work to do."

"It's a damn blizzard outside, Nora."

"It is?" She stands and walks into my office, staring out at the flurry of snow, whipping violently in the air. "Wow. It's a mess out there. There are no cars driving below. I don't know if I've ever seen that happen since I moved to the city."

"I should have sent you home hours ago. I'm sorry, I got caught up in here, and well, it's not a good excuse."

"I don't have any windows out there," she reminds me. "But I'm sure I'll get home okay."

I shove my hands in my pockets so I don't do something

stupid like brush my fingers through her hair. "I don't think either of us is leaving tonight."

"That's crazy."

"No, crazy is leaving in this mess. No one's on the street for a reason. Look at those snowdrifts."

"Well, damn it." She presses her forehead to the glass, watching the snow explode around us. "It's like a snow globe on steroids."

"Yeah, it kind of is."

"I guess I can go back to work, then."

"Why don't you shut it down for the night?"

"Because I'm stuck at work, so I might as well *work*?"

"Aren't you hungry?"

She stops to think about it. "Actually, I'm starving. I don't think I've eaten anything since the tea and muffin you brought me this morning."

I plant my hand on the small of her back—big mistake—and lead her out of my office, toward the kitchen.

"We'll find something. I would order in, but no one will deliver in this mess."

Once in the employee kitchen, Nora opens the fridge and I start opening cabinets.

"Dave the junior attorney has a science experiment in here," she says, wrinkling her nose. "Ew."

"There's got to be fresh stuff around here somewhere."

"I see a few freezer meals. Mostly Lean Cuisine."

"I think this bag of chips is from Cinco de Mayo," I reply, holding up a half-eaten bag of tortilla chips.

"It's November," she reminds me. "So those are probably stale."

We're both tossing spoiled food into the garbage, looks of disgust on our faces.

"This used to be soup. I think." She's examining a plastic container. "But I'm not hungry enough to open it."

"Toss it."

"Well, the fridge is clean now. I found some oranges and a leftover taco that looks fresh."

"I found packets of mustard, some ramen noodles, and a can of tomato soup."

"Didn't Quinn have a lunch brought in earlier today for clients?"

"Let's go see if there's anything left in the conference room."

We hurry down the hall and open the door.

"Cookies," Nora says with happiness. "And it looks like warm sandwiches. I don't want to get sick."

"We'll eat the cookies. There are bags of chips over here, too."

"My diet is ruined, but we won't starve," she says as she sits in one of the plush leather chairs and munches on a chocolate chip cookie.

"You don't need a diet."

"Psh, you don't see me naked."

She frowns at her cookie, as if she didn't mean to say that, and I sit next to her, at the head of the table.

I'd love to see you naked, sweetheart.

But that seems like something she *could* sue me for, so I keep it to myself and reach for a chocolate chip cookie.

I pull my phone out of my pocket and call Maggie, Quinn and Finn's mom.

"Hello, dear," she says when she answers.

"I'm just checking in on you and Gabby."

"Oh, we're right as rain. Just hunkered down, watching TV and eating some chili. Did you make it home okay?"

"No, I'm at work for the night."

"Well, don't worry about our Gabby girl. She's fine here."

"Thanks, Maggie. I'll call her before bedtime."

"You're welcome. Good night."

I hang up and reach for another cookie. "Thank God for Maggie."

"I like her," Nora says with a nod. "She's a kick in the pants, and Gabby sure loves being with her. I'm so glad the doctor figured out her medication issues earlier this year."

Maggie was on medicine that was giving her side effects that resembled dementia. But now she's on the right medicine and doing much better.

"Me, too. Scared us all."

We're quiet for a moment as we eat our cookies and listen to the wind howl outside.

"I hope the power doesn't go out," she says.

"Are you afraid of the dark?"

"Not really, I just don't want to lose internet. Something tells me we'll be streaming movies for entertainment tonight."

"You have a point." I snatch up the rest of the cookies, grab the basket of chips, and gesture toward my office. "Speaking of which, why don't we go back to my office where it's more comfortable."

"Okay."

I follow her down the hall, watching as her ass sways as she walks, her calves flex with the push and pull in those heels.

Jesus, she's beautiful. And I'm here, alone, with her all night.

It's going to kill me.

Chapter Three

~Nora~

I've eaten my weight in cookies." I lean back on the couch and pat my belly. "This is every seven-year-old's dream."

"If I ever see another Ruffle in my lifetime, it'll be too soon."

He's watching me from across the couch. He took off his tie and unfastened the top two buttons of his white shirt. His hair is messy, and he has the beginnings of dark stubble on his face.

I kick off my heels and sigh in relief. They don't usually bother me, but after sixteen hours of being trapped in them, my feet are begging for mercy.

"I called my mother today," Carter says with a sigh. He suddenly looks tired as he rubs his eyes with his fingers. "That went as well as expected."

"I'm sorry."

I've never met Carter's family, but I've had to take a few calls from them over the years. No one would use the phrase *warm and fuzzy* when describing his folks. I don't know the history there, but from what I gather, it's not good.

"It is what it is," he says and shrugs one shoulder. "Are you close to your family? Why don't I know anything about them?"

I smile. "Because I'm your assistant."

"But you know about my family."

"Bits and pieces," I concede. "But not everything. To answer your question, no. I'm not close with my family. I'm an only child."

This piques his interest, and he turns toward me more fully, pulling one leg on the cushion and bracing his head on his hand, his elbow planted on the back of the couch.

"Me, too," he says softly.

"I guess you could say my parents don't exactly agree with my life choices," I continue, and he nods, as if he completely understands.

"My parents didn't like Darcy, and they hate that I became an attorney."

"Wait. Your parents hate that their only son became an übersuccessful lawyer in New York City?"

"I was supposed to be a surgeon, like my father and his father before him."

"Ah. You strayed."

"Big-time," he agrees. "And Darcy didn't come from an influential southern family, so she was immediately unlikable."

"Well, that sucks, and it's their loss."

"That's what I think, too." He smiles kindly. "Do your parents not approve of you working for an übersuccessful attorney in New York City?"

I lean my head back on the couch, thinking it over. "It's not that. I know they'd rather I was home in Cleveland, but living here doesn't really bother them."

"What is it, then?"

"Oh, they hate that I divorced Richard."

He narrows his eyes at me. "Why?"

"Because divorce is a no-no in my family. I should have been a dutiful wife and sucked it up. But eff that. Life's too short to suck it up."

"You're completely right," he agrees and clears his throat. "Are you back in the dating game yet?"

I shake my head slowly. "Who has time to date when you work for an übersuccessful attorney?"

"Or *are* an attorney," he mutters.

"How about you?"

"Same boat. I did go out on one date, but it was a disaster. I don't think I'm good at it."

"You can't be that bad."

"I'm out of practice," he admits. "I'd most likely fumble my way through and embarrass everyone."

"You're not giving yourself enough credit." I laugh and tuck my feet under me, getting more comfortable on the couch. "I've known you for a long time, Carter. You're a charming man. I'm sure you'd be a fun date."

Not to mention, you're sexy as hell. Getting caught here all night with him was not the best idea for my libido. Not that I did it on purpose. But damn it, I just want to crawl on top of him and have my way with him.

And he's looking at me with curious blue eyes, but there's nothing at all in his body language that screams *DO ME*.

So I'll stay on my side of the couch and keep my incredibly awesome job intact.

"Maybe you should go out for dinner with me," he suggests. "Give me some pointers, make sure I'm not making a complete ass of myself."

Ah, a trial run, go with someone he knows and trusts to see if he's doing it right. A friends-only date.

Which is exactly what it should be.

Because I love my job, and Christopher is right; workplace romances never work out.

Maybe this is what I need. Get Carter back in the dating game, and maybe it'll propel me forward in my own love life.

"You don't have to—"

"Good idea," I say at the same time. "I'll totally go on a date with you."

He quirks an eyebrow. "You will?"

"Sure. You'll see, it's not nearly as bad as you think it is. When should we go?"

"Tomorrow. After work." It's not a question. "And as your boss, I insist you leave at a normal time tomorrow so we can eat dinner like normal human beings."

"I have to pick Gabby up for piano lessons," I remind him.

"Perfect. Don't come back to the office when you're done."

"Yes, sir."

His lips turn up in a small smile. "Whenever you're ready to sleep, Finn has a queen-size bed off his office. He had it built on because he slept here more than at his house back before he met London."

"Where will you sleep?"

"On this couch."

"I can take the couch."

He tips his head. "No. I'll take the couch."

"If you say so. Do you want me to leave so you can sleep?"

"I'm fine if you are."

"Yeah, I'm a night owl. I still have a couple of hours in me. Should we watch a movie?"

"Sure. What movie should we watch?"

"Something funny. And romantic. *Crazy Rich Asians.*"

"Yes, ma'am."

"Why are you going out with my dad?" Gabby asks the following afternoon when I'm driving her home from her lesson. Mother Nature calmed down a bit through the day today, but there's still a lot of snow out here, so I'm white-knuckling it, maneuvering my way through Manhattan.

Why was I so stubborn about keeping my car in the city? We are *not* in the Midwest.

"Do you have a business meeting?" she continues.

"No, we're just going out for dinner."

"Like, on a date?"

I can feel her blue eyes pinned to me, and I'm not sure how to answer the question.

"Sort of, but only as friends."

"Why as friends? You could totally date my dad. I actually *like* you."

"Well, thanks. I think. But there is a whole laundry list of reasons why I shouldn't date your dad for real."

"Like what? Tell me the reasons so I can debunk them."

I laugh and glance over at the preteen. "Debunk?"

"Yeah, you know, prove why it's wrong."

"I know what it means. Well, Gabs, I work for your dad. And we have rules in the office that people aren't supposed to date each other."

"My dad owns the company," she reminds me with confidence. "So he can change the rules."

"It's really not a bad rule. Because when people date in the workplace, it can get messy if things don't work out."

"Because people are dumb," she says with a sage nod. "So dramatic. But my dad is *not* dramatic. So I don't think it'll be an issue."

"I'm so glad to hear that." I chuckle and pull into Maggie's driveway. Gabby usually spends evenings with her grandmother, and both look forward to it. "Have a good night tonight."

"I'm just saying, if you're into my dad, I'm cool with it. And trust me when I say, I wouldn't say that to just anyone."

"That means a lot, Gabs. I mean it. Thank you, but I think this is just a casual dinner as friends."

"Fine." She sighs heavily and pushes out of the car, hurrying through the snow to the front door. Maggie opens the door for her and they both wave at me before hurrying inside, out of the cold.

I would usually go back to the office now, but Carter made it clear that was off the table for today. He's picking me up at six sharp, so I don't really have time to go back and work at this point anyway. I have ninety minutes to take a shower and put myself together for our date.

Our pseudodate, that is.

Because it's not real.

And I'd better remember that.

Fighting my way back into Manhattan takes a bit longer than normal thanks to the weather, but the fact that my parking space is open for me is a huge win these days. Not to mention, the elevator is fixed.

Hot damn.

Once in my apartment, I walk directly through my bedroom to the small walk-in closet and ponder my outfit choices.

I mostly have work clothes because, let's face it, that's usually where I am. My wardrobe consists of suits and yoga pants, with little in between.

Until this very moment, that wasn't a problem.

"I have a little black dress," I murmur, running my fingers over the material. "But it's kind of cliché, isn't it? This blue dress is pretty."

I tap my chin. "But the weather is awful. I'll freeze my tits off in the blue dress because I don't have a jacket to match. I can wear almost anything with the black. Black it is."

I choose a simple pair of black pumps and a red clutch to go with it, and then head for the shower.

I now have fifty-five minutes until Carter shows up. No time to waste.

When I'm buffed and polished, wearing the simple but classic outfit, and after I smooth on some red lipstick to match my clutch, the buzzer at the front door rings.

Perfect timing. I buzz him up and finish primping, then hurry to the front door.

I pull open the door, and there's Carter, in a navy blue suit with a pale pink button-down, and a wool overcoat on to fight the cold. His eyes roam up and down my body, and when they reach mine, he offers me a full smile, showing off that crazy dimple in his left cheek.

"You're beautiful."

He's supposed to say that. It's a practice date.

"Thank you, kind sir." I step back to usher him inside and am shocked when he pulls a bouquet of white roses from behind his back. "For me?"

"You're the only date here," he says and chuckles when I bury my nose in the blooms and take a deep breath.

"They're gorgeous. Thank you. Give me two seconds to put these in water, and I'm ready to go."

"No hurry," he assures me and follows me to the kitchen.

"Gabby told me all about helping you decorate this living room."

"Well, you know we love us some Joanna Gaines. And I decided to give the place a farmhouse feel. Gabby was a big help."

"She was so proud of it," he agrees. "She showed me photos on her phone, but it doesn't do it justice. Your home looks great."

I smile, genuinely happy that he likes my place. I've worked hard to make it comfortable and stylish. Richard always hated it when I "wasted money" on pretty things for our home.

"Thanks." I set the bouquet of flowers on the coffee table. "Ready when you are."

"Let's go then."

He surprises me by taking my hand in his and leading me out of the apartment to the elevator. His hand is warm and strong. He rubs the pad of his thumb along the side of my hand and it sends goose bumps over my arms.

It's probably better for my own sanity if we don't spend all night touching, but I can't seem to find the courage to pull away. Not because I'm afraid but because *it feels so damn good*.

"I hope you're hungry," Carter says as we begin our descent to the lobby.

"Superhungry, and hoping we get more than cookies this evening. My old lady stomach just can't do that two days in a row."

He laughs and shakes his head. "I was thinking steak."

"I like the way you think."

He hails a cab and we're off, not having far to go to reach a nearby steakhouse. If it were summer, we could easily walk it.

Carter's hand is on the small of my back as we follow the hostess to our table, situated in an intimate corner of the dimly lit restaurant.

Once we're seated with drinks and our order placed, Carter sighs and holds my hand in his, pulling it up to his lips, pressing a soft kiss to my knuckles.

Jesus, Mary, and Joseph, he's laying this whole pretend date on thick.

If I were a real date, I'd be counting the minutes until date number two.

I don't know what he was worried about.

"I can't believe you had time to go home and change before picking me up," I say, attempting to calm my damn pulse and pull it together.

"I brought a change of clothes with me," he admits with a smile.

"You got something past me!"

"I know, I was shocked. You don't see *everything*."

"Hmm." I usually do, but I've been distracted today. "Well, I like the blue suit. You look nice in it."

"I'll wear it every day, if it makes you happy."

I laugh and take a sip of my red wine. "You might want to just rotate it through. But it looks nice."

"I don't think I've ever seen you in anything but a suit."

He has, he just doesn't remember. Which is a reminder at how little he's noticed about me in the past.

"It would most likely be frowned upon to wear jeans to work."

"We could do casual Fridays," he suggests, but I shake my head.

"I think if a client is paying millions for his attorney, the staff should look professional."

"You're probably right," he replies, and we sit back as our dinner is served, forced to pull our hands away from each other.

We're quiet as we eat, both of us hungry and the food delicious.

"Would you like some dessert?" the waitress asks when she clears away our empty dinner plates.

"Oh, I couldn't," I reply.

"We have tiramisu tonight," she says, and I cave.

"Sold. I'll take it."

"Me, too," Carter says with a nod.

"Oh, you can share mine. Please don't make me eat the whole thing by myself."

"Are you sure?"

"Yes. Absolutely."

He looks up at the waitress. "Just one dessert then."

"Coming right up."

She bustles away and Carter reaches for my hand again.

"I wouldn't have figured you for a physically affectionate person," I say, thinking aloud.

"I think there's plenty about both of us that we don't know," he says and I nod in agreement.

A working relationship is very different from a romantic one.

And after tonight, we'll go back to the way it's always been.

He's my boss. This is just a pretend date, even though it feels quite real from where I'm sitting.

"Here you go," the waitress says as she sets a large square of tiramisu in front of us, with two clean forks. "Enjoy."

"Holy shit," I murmur. "I'm so glad you agreed to share this."

"It's delicious," he says after taking the first bite. "I probably didn't need to know this existed."

"Why?"

"Because I'll order just this for takeout way too often."

"Oh, I hadn't thought of doing that. Genius idea. And dangerous."

We gobble up the delicious dessert, and once Carter has settled the bill, we walk out of the restaurant and he hails a cab to take us back to my place.

"This is it," he says to the cabdriver. "Do you mind waiting for me while I walk the lady to her door?"

"I'll wait," he replies, and I shake my head.

"You don't have to—"

"I'm walking you up," he insists and follows me out of the car and inside, then up the elevator.

Once at my door, he pins me against the wall, one hand braced above my head and the other cupping my cheek.

Holy hell, he's potent. Tall and firm. He smells amazing, and his eyes are hot on mine.

"I had a good time," I say with a thick voice.

"I'm glad," he murmurs. "I had the best evening I've had in quite some time."

He's leaning in closer, and the next thing I know, his lips are on mine. Soft, tender. His thumb is making circles on my cheek.

I could lose myself in this man. Every female gene is screaming for me to invite him inside so we can see where this incredible kiss can go.

But it's not real.

He pulls back slowly and licks his lips.

"Good night, Nora."

"Night."

He waits while I unlock my door and step inside, and then I hear his footsteps down the hall to the elevator, and I lean against the door in relief.

That was the best date of my life.

It's a pity that it wasn't real.

I MADE SOME decisions last night, while I tossed and turned in bed, not able to get that kiss out of my sex-deprived head.

It was pathetic, really.

Carter is totally ready to date. His skills are on point, and if he just does things the way he did last night, he'll have women lined up around the block to get a chance to go out with him.

Do I love the thought? Admittedly no. But it needs to happen. Carter *needs* to date so I can get the ridiculous notion that I'm attracted to him out of my head.

I will be mature and an adult about the matter. I will only be a little jealous of the tramp that snags him for the long haul.

I mean nice woman. Not tramp.

See? I'm mature.

So I made a list of some of the people I know who might be good fits for Carter, just to get him started.

Okay, the list has three names on it because I don't know that many people, but it's something.

As I'm walking into the office, I'm surprised to see through the open door that Carter is already in his office, with Finn and Quinn sitting with him.

Now's as good of a time as any.

I walk into the room, and all conversation stops.

"Good morning," I say brightly.

"Good morning, Nora," Carter says with a smile.

"I'm sorry to interrupt," I say. "I just wanted to stop in before the workday gets under way, since this is *not* work related, and say that you did so well last night, Carter. You've got this dating thing in the bag. You're charming and interesting and seriously, any girl would be lucky to date you.

"And in that vein, I went ahead and made a short list of nice women I know who you might want to call."

I pass him the paper and then wipe my sweaty palms on my skirt as all three men look at one another in surprise, their mouths gaping open.

"See? Dating isn't so hard. Okay, guys, have a good day."

I hurry out of his office and shut the door behind me, then let out a gusty sigh.

I sounded like a complete buffoon.

But it had to happen.

Chapter Four

~Carter~

*W*hat. The fuck. Just happened.

"Uh, Carter?" Finn asks, scooting to the edge of his seat and bracing his elbows on his knees, looking at me with a furrowed brow and confusion written all over his face.

I just finished telling both of my brothers-in-law about last night's successful date.

It *was* successful.

Or so I thought.

"I don't know," I reply without him voicing the rest of his question.

"Did you make her think you were going out on a *friend* date?" Quinn asks incredulously.

"I don't think so." I stand and shove my hands in my pockets.

"What, exactly, did you say when you asked her out?"

How the hell do I know? I was nervous as hell. She was sitting three feet from me looking sexy as all get-out, and I was doing my damnedest to not pull her under me and have my way with her.

I pace behind my desk, trying to think back to the night Nora and I were stuck in the office. "We were talking about getting back in the dating saddle, and I admitted that I'm not very good at it."

"Understatement," Finn mutters, earning a glare from me. "Go on."

"And she said that I couldn't be that bad, and I suggested *she* go to dinner with me."

"As what, a practice date?" Quinn asks.

"No, I—" I pause and lean on the back of my desk chair, then hang my head. "Jesus, I'm a dumbass."

"You said it," Finn says cheerfully.

"This is a lost cause," I say. "Nora's never going to see me as anything but her boss. And frankly, that's probably how it *should* be."

"Listen, Nora's the first woman who has turned your head even a little bit since Darcy died," Quinn says. "And take my word for it, she likes you, too."

"Clearly. She just marched in here and gave me a list of women to date. *Nora* is not on this list."

"She's scared," Finn says quietly. "And who can blame her? She ran out of here like a frightened bunny."

"I'm hardly terrifying."

"You can be," Quinn says. "I've seen you work a courtroom. Hell, I've *heard* you yell at clients from my office."

"And you're not a yeller," Finn adds. "You can be intense, but you're also kind and, I agree, not scary. I don't think she's scared of *you*, she's afraid of what could happen if this were to go further."

"You guys should have been psychologists, not attorneys," I say as I sit in my chair with a sigh.

"You have to court her," Finn continues. "I know it sounds old-fashioned, but that's what it is. You need to show her that you're interested. Make an effort."

"Flowers," Quinn suggests. "Small gestures that show you pay attention to her. Show her that you're interested."

"Sex therapists instead of attorneys."

"Funny." Finn stands and Quinn follows suit. "If Nora's the one you want—"

"Without question."

Both men smile down at me.

"Then go earn her," Quinn says with a wink. "You may be rusty, but you've got this."

"I've got a meeting," Finn says, checking the time. "Keep us posted."

"A couple of gossiping hens," I mutter as I wake up my computer and search for a local florist.

It's been a hell of a day. I had two unexpected meetings and a panicked client, all before noon. I've barely had time to step out of my office to see Nora.

Which is pretty typical, but today I'm aching for her. Which is ridiculous because apparently she couldn't wait to pawn me off on a "friend."

I can't believe that she could misunderstand last night as anything other than a real date. I was attentive. Affectionate. We laughed and talked about topics other than work.

That kiss at her door made me want to hit my knees and beg for more.

The chemistry between us is *there.* And I'm convinced that she has to feel it, too.

Is Finn right? Is she afraid?

There's a knock on my office door.

"Come in."

Nora opens the door and pokes her pretty blond head inside. When she opens the door wider, she's holding a bouquet of white roses in one hand, and the card in another.

"This is a *really* fancy way to call me into your office."

I smile and gesture to the seat in front of my desk. "Come have a seat."

"Shall I shut this behind me?"

"Yes, please."

She does as I ask and sets the vase of blooms on the side of my desk and takes a seat, gazing at me expectantly. "What's up?"

"I want to talk about this." I hold the sheet of paper she gave me this morning up between my forefinger and thumb.

"My list?"

"Yes. Your list." I hold her gaze in mine as I reach down and send the paper through the shredder. Her eyes widen as the loud whirling of the tearing paper fills the air, and when it's done she clears her throat.

"So I guess you didn't like that list."

"No." I lean on the desk and fold my hands. "I didn't like it. I don't plan to use it. Today, or ever."

"I can probably think up other names—"

"Unless *Nora* is on the list, I'm not interested," I interrupt and watch in fascination as her face flushes. I've known this woman for a long time, and I don't ever recall seeing her flustered before.

I like it. I can't wait to see her face flushed like this when she's under me and begging for mercy.

"The only Nora I know is . . . me." The last word is said in a sexy, disbelieving whisper. I want to kiss her, here and now.

Instead, I grin at her and her brown eyes fall to my left cheek. She's been doing that for a couple of months now.

"That's right. You. Nora, I don't intend to date anyone from a list you make for me, or anyone you *don't* put on a list. I'm interested in seeing more of you. I thought I made that pretty clear last night, and I'm sorry if that's not the case."

"I had a good time last night," she says, her eyes not moving from mine. "But I'd pretty much convinced myself that it was all for the sake of a practice date."

"Practice dates don't include hand-holding or kisses at your front door."

She presses her lips together, as if she's remembering the taste of my mouth on hers.

It's a damn sexy sight.

"Do you honestly think that I'm not interested in you?"

"I don't know what to think," she admits and closes her eyes briefly. "This is all so . . . odd. Carter, I've worked for you for years, and honestly, I love my job. I can't do anything that could jeopardize my position here because I enjoy it. I'm good at it. And frankly, I need it."

"I know." I nod and glance down at my hands. "I've given this some thought. Nora, you'd never lose your job here if a personal relationship between us didn't work."

"But it would be so *awkward* if it doesn't," she insists. "You can say that, but let's say we date for a year, have all the crazy sex in the world and fall in love with each other, and then decide to go our separate ways? We can't do that because I'll still be here, every day, in your business."

"Let's go back to the crazy sex," I suggest, making her snort laugh.

"I'm serious."

"I know you are, and you're not wrong to worry. Here's what I know for sure: I'm completely attracted to you. And in addition to that, I enjoy you. We have great conversations, and you make me laugh. I just enjoy being with you. There's nothing wrong with spending some extra time together outside of work, Nora."

"I just hate the idea of being the topic of office gossip." She bites her lip. "I stay away from office drama."

"That's one of the many things I like about you."

She chews that lip as she watches me for a long moment. Just when I think she's going to tell me to go fuck myself, she says, "Okay, if we're going to do this, there has to be rules."

"Should we make another list?"

"Excellent idea." She grabs a pad of scratch paper and pen from my desk for notes. "First, we have to act like nothing personal is happening between us when we're here. No hanky-panky. No coming and going together."

"There is so much innuendo in that statement, I don't even know where to start."

She raises a brow like I'm an insolent child and makes me laugh.

"Focus here, Carter."

"Fine. No, how did you put it? Hanky-panky."

She makes a note.

"No more giving me lists of women to date," I say. "That's an important rule."

She chuckles and makes the note. "I can live with that. I didn't love making that list. I thought I was being helpful. Okay, I guess we can start there and add to it if we think of other things."

"I have another rule," I add.

"Okay, shoot."

She's looking down at the paper, pen poised to jot down what I'm about to say.

God, she's amazing.

"You have to wear those black shoes with the red bows on the heels at least once a week."

Her gaze whips up to mine.

"You like those?"

"I like you in all your heels, but the red bows are an extra-special touch."

She smiles and tilts her head to the side, watching me.

"I'll be happy to wear them. You know, I have a thing for the new navy slacks you bought not long ago."

I arch a brow. "Is that so?"

"Oh yeah. They . . . fit nicely."

"I'll remember that." We sit, smiling at each other. "Are we flirting with each other right now?"

"It seems we are, and that's against rule number one."

"Meh, we can bend the rules a bit. I like flirting with you."

She sets the paper and pad aside.

"Dinner," I continue. "Tomorrow night. I would say tonight, but I promised Gabby we'd go to the movies."

"I can do that, but I can't leave the office early again."

"We'll go from here."

"Okay." She nods. "But what about Gabby?"

"Tomorrow's Friday. She's staying with Maggie. She's been spending extra time with her grandmother lately."

"Okay, then. Is there anything else you need right now?"

Yes. I need to pull you against me and kiss you until you can't breathe.

But that would be blurring rule number one too much, especially for the first day.

"I think that's all."

"Well, then, I'll be expecting another bouquet of flowers the next time you need to see me in your office."

She winks as she stands, lifts her flowers, and sashays out of my office, closing the door behind her.

And I begin counting the hours until I can get her alone.

"THAT WAS *SO good*," Gabby says as we walk out of the theater to my car.

"I'm glad you're not too old for animated movies," I say as I buckle my seat belt. "Because I like them, too."

"The funny ones are great," she says. "Also, we should get a dog."

I stare at her in surprise. "How did we go from movies to dogs?"

"I'm just saying," she says calmly, making me smile. My daughter is smart, way smarter than I sometimes give her credit for. And now that her behavior issues from last year seem to be resolved, she's fun to be around again.

She's the best.

"Gabs, you know we're not home enough to have a dog. They need constant care. I wish we could make it work, but it just doesn't seem fair."

"I'm home way more than you are," she reminds me. "And besides, it can stay with Grandma when we're not home. I'm at Grandma's a lot anyway."

"We are *not* saddling your grandmother with a dog she doesn't want." My voice is firm, the one that says this is not up for discussion.

"Dad, I talked to Grandma about it, and she said she'd be up for it. A dog would be a great companion for her when she's alone."

I sigh and rub my hand over my mouth as I drive us home. "I'll have to talk with her about it, Gabs."

"Oh my gosh, does this mean you'll think about it?"

"It means I'm going to talk to Maggie about it. Don't get your hopes up because I do *not* think this is the best idea."

"Okay. I won't. Honest. But if you say yes, I'll totally take care of it. You won't have to do *anything*."

"Famous last words," I mutter as I park and lead Gabby up to our penthouse. I owned a house with Darcy, still do actually, but I haven't been able to live there since she passed.

There are just too many difficult memories there.

I should sell the house, but I haven't been able to do that, either.

So Gabby and I live in this penthouse in Manhattan, which is big and modern. More than comfortable.

"Can I stay up to watch Netflix?"

"No, ma'am. You have school in the morning. Go take your shower and get ready for bed."

"Darn it."

"Actually, hold on a second. Let's have a chat."

"I swear, I haven't done anything."

I laugh and kiss the top of her head. "I know. I just want to talk to you for a minute."

"Okay." She sits on the couch and pulls her legs up under her, waiting expectantly.

"Gabby, I want to know what you think about the idea of me starting to date."

She frowns. "Uh, I think it's gross."

"Because you're afraid I'll try to replace your mother?"

"No, because you'll probably have sex and stuff, and that's disgusting."

I laugh, covering my eyes with my hand. Yep, she's hilarious. Then, my head snaps up. "Wait. What do you know about sex?"

Gabby rolls her eyes and sighs deeply as if I'm the dumbest man on the planet. "Dad, I'm twelve. I'm not stupid."

"You're the smartest person I know," I reply immediately, meaning every word. "But you're *only* twelve, and I should know how much you think you know."

"I took health class." She shrugs one shoulder. "They explained the basics, and it sounds gross."

"It is. Keep thinking that. It's awful. Horrible. And something you do when you're thirty."

She giggles now. "You're weird. I don't care if you date. I don't think. Unless it's someone dumb. I mean, you can't date someone that I hate."

"Obviously."

"Because my friend Sara's mom starting dating this total douche nozzle. No douche nozzles."

"I think we can manage that. In fact"—I clear my throat—"I would like to start dating Nora."

Her whole face breaks out into a big smile. "It's about time! Dad, Nora's awesome."

"I know."

"I told her the other day that she should date you, but she said it's complicated."

"Well, it is a little complicated," I concede. "But I like her very much, and I'd like to spend more time with her outside of work."

"I can spend more time with Grandma," my sweet daughter offers, and I tug her into my arms for a hug.

"I think we'll invite you to come with us most of the time, Gabs. You're my daughter, my family, and if I'm dating *any* woman, she'll need to get to know you, too."

"But you're going to want to do romantic stuff, and that's not my idea of a good time."

"Yes, I hope to have some romantic times, but we'll have lots of times when we're just hanging out, and there's no reason that you can't be with us."

"Yeah, I guess that could be fun," she says. "I'm happy for you, Dad."

I stare at my daughter. She's growing up so fast. Way quicker than I'm comfortable with. And she looks just like her mother.

Darcy loved her, and it makes me sad that Gabby is missing out on having her mother as she grows up.

"Are you okay, Gabs?"

"I told you, I like Nora."

"I don't just mean that. I mean, are you generally okay?"

She sighs and sits back against the cushions. "Yeah. I'd be better if I could watch Netflix tonight with my new dog—"

"Don't push it."

"I'm good. Thanks for asking me if I'm okay with the gross dating."

"We're a team, baby girl. We need to be on the same page or this doesn't work."

"Like last year, when I was such a royal brat."

"You were just a little brat."

She laughs. "Hormones."

"What, exactly, do you know about hormones?"

Gabby groans as she shoves her face in a pillow and says, "Daaaaad."

"What? I need to know these things."

"I love you, Dad."

"I love you, too, Gabs."

"So about Netflix."

"Nope."

"I had to try."

Chapter Five

~Nora~

Good morning, Nora," Carter says in greeting as he walks into the office Friday morning. He's wearing those navy blue slacks I told him I like, and that left dimple is firmly in place as he grins and places a manila folder on my desk. "I have some notes for the Dickinson case I need you to look over right away."

I frown up at him. He *never* asks me to look over case notes. Well, unless he's asking me to fetch them or file them away.

But read them? No.

"Uh, okay."

"Great. Have a good day, Nora."

And with that, he walks into his office and shuts the door, just like any other normal day.

Confused, I open the folder and find a handwritten note from Carter.

> *N—*
>
> *We said to act normal at work, so this is the only way I could come up with to send personal messages back and forth. I'm looking forward to our date this evening. And if I haven't told you yet today, you look fantastic.*

He wrote this before he even saw what I was wearing today. Carter Shaw is a charmer.

> *I hope you have a great day. The hours will creep by for me.*
>
> *—C*

I did *not* expect this. Flirty notes that we pass back and forth in this folder seems a bit childish, but exciting at the same time.

We can't email back and forth because that leaves a trail. We could just text—that would be easier—but this is sort of old-fashioned and tantalizing. And the fact that Carter was creative enough to come up with it sets the butterflies in my belly into full flutter.

I tuck the note in my purse and pull out a blank piece of paper.

C—

Thank you for coming up with such a fun way to communicate during the day. It's kind of sexy that you thought of it. I see you're wearing my favorite slacks today.

I'm also excited for our date. What time should I be ready to go for the day?

TGIF!

—N

I tuck the note into the folder and walk into Carter's office.

"I read over your notes and added my own, for you to read at your convenience."

I pass him the folder and immediately turn to walk back to my desk.

On my way out the door, I whisper to myself, "I hope you know what you're doing, Nora.

"Hey, Sienna," I say when I see the attorney standing at my desk. "What can I do for you?"

"I need a full-time assistant," she says with a sigh. "I thought I could get through a couple of weeks without one, but my plate is already full, and I don't feel comfortable calling on you all the time. You have your own full-time job."

"Okay, let's take a look at the résumés that have come in from the staffing service and see what we have."

"Thank you," she says with a smile. "Meet me in my office whenever you're free."

"I'll be there in fifteen minutes."

"You're the best," she says with a grateful smile and walks back toward her office, down the hall from her husband's. Quinn wanted her close. Not because he thinks he has to help her, or save her from anything. He knows Sienna is more than capable of taking care of herself.

No, he just loves her to distraction and wanted her to be nearby. It's romantic and sweet.

Two words I never would have used to describe Quinn in the past. He's always been kind to me, but he's the reckless one. The *bad boy*. And now, with Sienna, he's still edgy with a soft spot for the woman he's crazy about.

I'm happy for him.

Just as I'm gathering my laptop and supplies to take into Sienna's office, my phone pings with a text from Carter.

I'll meet you in the parking garage at 6:00.

I send him back a quick reply and then call him on the office phone to let him know I'll be with Sienna for a bit.

Today is going to be the longest day of my life.

"I'm so dang full," I say with a sigh as I pat my belly. "If this is going to be the norm when we go out on dates, I'll need to start some sort of rigorous cardio routine. And, frankly, I don't like to sweat."

Carter laughs and reaches for my hand. "You don't like to *sweat*?"

"No. I don't. It's just . . . sweaty."

"So noted," he replies. "I plan to feed you well, Nora. I plan to do a lot of things well."

If that doesn't send a zing down my spine and straight to my lady parts, I don't know what does.

I cross my legs, here in his car, trying to relieve the pressure between them.

"Are you okay?" he asks.

"Fine. Just fine. And full. Thanks for dinner. One of these nights, I'd like to cook for you."

"Do you like to cook?"

"I love it, I just don't usually have a lot of time for it. I cook for Gabby and me a lot when I have her on the weekends, but now that she's spending more time with Maggie, I haven't been doing that, either."

"She never said that you cook," he murmurs. "I suddenly feel like I've missed out on a lot of time with you and Gabby."

"Like we're off having fun without you?" I grin over at him and watch the way the street lights flicker over his handsome face as we drive. "It's okay. We have time."

He reaches for my hand and gives it a squeeze. "I'm glad."

His hand is warm and strong, with long fingers that seem to dwarf my own hand. But it fits me perfectly.

"Come home with me," he says softly. "I'm not ready to say good night, and Gabby's not home."

"I'd like that," I reply immediately, not even pretending to be coy. There's no need with Carter. "But my car is at the office."

"We'll go get it tomorrow." He raises the back of my hand to his lips. "I'm impatient to finally be alone with you."

"You've been alone with me all evening."

"No, we were in a restaurant full of other people," he counters and kisses my hand once more before letting go to put both hands on the wheel. "And now I get to have you to myself."

It's both odd and thrilling, sitting in Carter's car, hearing him say romantic words. Unexpected.

Sexy.

And it's about to get a whole lot sexier.

He parks and leads me up to his penthouse. I've been here plenty of times in the past, with Gabby, dropping off dinners, fetching or delivering this and that.

But this is new. I helped Carter pick this place out, back when he was still grief-stricken and trying to find a home for him and his daughter that didn't remind him of his late wife. He told me to pick out five places, and we toured each of them together.

It came down to this one.

It was my favorite and he didn't really care at the time. It's an open floor plan, with a beautiful kitchen that I know he hardly uses.

Man, the meals I could cook in that kitchen.

But we don't make it as far as the kitchen. Once inside the front door, I set my bag on the table and kick out of my shoes, and Carter rounds on me, his blue eyes pinning mine before he presses his body against me, pushing me against the wall.

"If this is too much, say so now."

I'm breathing hard, and staring up into his bright blue eyes, already yearning for him.

"Not too much," I whisper, just before he brushes his lips across my own. His touch is light, completely opposite of the intensity in his eyes and his taut muscles.

His hands frame my jaw, fingers brushing into my hair, and I'm immediately lost in him. In the feel of his hands on me, his hypnotizing lips.

Holy shit, this man is potent.

He grazes one hand down my shoulder to my breast and cups it over the fabric of my blouse and bra. My nipple puckers, making us both moan in delight.

"You're so damn sweet," he groans, but before he can do anything else, the phone in his pocket rings. He fumbles for his phone and frowns at the display. "It's Maggie."

"You'd better answer it."

He pauses, gazing down at me with hot eyes, then pulls back and accepts the call.

"Hey, Maggie." His brows shoot down in a frown. "You're kidding me."

He drags his hand down his face and looks over at me with regret.

Our night is over.

"Of course you did the right thing. Yes, I'm on my way. No,

it's okay. Sure, put her on. Hi, sweetheart. I'm so sorry you're sick. Yes, I'm coming to get you right now. You didn't ruin anything." He smiles now. "Don't worry, okay? I'll see you in a little bit."

He hangs up and turns to me.

"What's wrong?" I ask immediately. "What's wrong with Gabby?"

"Chicken pox," he says and shakes his head. "Maggie took her to urgent care, just to be sure. My kid has the chicken pox."

"Oh, the poor thing." I reach for my purse. "You go pick her up and I'll go to the pharmacy for supplies and meet you back here."

I'm tugged into Carter's arms, in a strong hug. "You don't have to stay."

"If you'd rather I didn't—"

"That's not what I said," he replies quickly. "You're welcome to stay, if you've already had the chicken pox."

"I did. And I'm happy to stay and help. Taking care of a sick kiddo isn't easy."

"Are you sure? I'm sorry, this isn't how I envisioned tonight going."

I laugh and then shrug. "That makes two of us, but yes, I'm sure. Let me help you."

"You're always helping me." His smile falls and he reaches out to brush his thumb over the apple of my cheek. "Who helps you, Nora?"

"I think that's a conversation for another time," I say. "Go get your daughter. I'll probably beat you back here."

"You don't have a car."

"The pharmacy is literally around the block. I'll be fine."

"Thank you."

"You're welcome."

We've had a break in the weather, so I don't have to try to make my way through snow in my heels on the short walk around the corner to the pharmacy. I immediately reach for the usual suspects: antihistamine, Tylenol for pain and fever, Gatorade, and chocolate.

Because chocolate is always necessary.

I also throw a couple of teen magazines in the basket, and on my way to the checkout counter, I see a set of oven mitts, covered in green ivy. They look like something my mother would have in her kitchen, and I snatch them up, remembering an episode of one of my favorite TV shows.

I was right. I beat them home. So I go straight to Gabby's room and put clean sheets on her queen-size bed. I put the magazines, medicine, and Gatorade on the bedside table, as well as the oven mitts, along with a small roll of tape I found.

Just as I get the pillowcases back on Gabby's pillows, I hear the front door open and footsteps down the hall to the bedroom.

"You did beat us back," Carter says.

"I have all the supplies you should need," I inform Gabby while I pull her in for a gentle hug. "I'm so sorry this happened, sweetie."

"I itch," she says. "And I'm hot."

"Fever," I murmur, feeling her head. "Did anyone give her anything for the fever?"

"Yes, she just had a Tylenol and a Benadryl. They should kick in soon," Carter says. "Gabs, why don't you put some pajamas on and get in bed?"

"Okay. Uh, what are the oven mitts for? Am I supposed to bake in my condition? Also, I think Grandma has the same ones."

I laugh and slide them on her hands. "I once saw an episode of *Friends*, where most of the cast gets the chicken pox. To keep from scratching, they duct-tape oven mitts on their hands. So if you get out of control scratching these things, we'll do the same thing."

"But if they itch, I should scratch them."

"No, if you scratch them, they'll bleed, and you'll scar." I lift my shirt up to show her my stomach. "See this? It's a chicken pox scar."

"But it *itches*."

"Trust me, I know." I pull some pajamas out of her dresser. The softest ones I can find. "Pull these on, and get settled."

"Dad, I know it makes me sound like a baby, but will you tuck me in?"

"Sure."

"And I want my letter from Mom." She bats her eyelashes, and Carter opens the bedside table drawer, pulling out a folded letter that's seen better days. It's been folded and unfolded a hundred times from the look of the battered creases.

"Here you go."

"Also," Gabby continues, "I'm not sleepy."

"That Benadryl will soon make you sleepy," Carter says as we leave the room. Then he says to me, "Thank you, for all this."

"It's my pleasure. Really. I'll wait in the living room while you tuck her in."

I make a pit stop in the kitchen and pour us each a glass of Carter's favorite wine, then make my way to his living room. As I get comfortable on the couch, I stare out at the city lit up beyond the windows. New York sure is pretty at night.

I've had a few sips of wine when Carter comes into the room and collapses on the couch with a sigh.

"She should fall asleep soon. She was reading one of the magazines you brought her."

"Good. Sleep will do her good. What's up with the letter?"

Carter sighs and sips his wine. "Darcy left a stack of letters for Gabby to read throughout the rest of her life. This one is for when she's feeling sick. There are letters for when she graduates from high school, college, gets married, has babies."

"Oh," I say and blink away tears. "That's actually really beautiful."

I want to ask if she left any letters for him, but before I can, he grins, showing me that dimple.

"So." He reaches for me and tugs me over to him. "Show me this scar again."

"You want to see my scar?"

"I want to see more than that, but let's start there."

I grin and straddle him on the couch, then lift my shirt to show him the tiny mark on my skin. His hands cradle my ass, and the next thing I know, he's leaning in to kiss me, right over the scar.

Damn, this man is intoxicating.

His hands move up, under my shirt and over my flesh as his lips take a tour of my ribs, and the tender underside of my breasts. Just as he reaches back to unfasten my bra, we hear, "Daaaaaad!"

"Shit," he whispers, pressing his face to my stomach.

"It's probably for the best."

"I know. I'm not going to make love to you for the first time when my kid is here."

I grin just as Gabby lets out another loud "Daaaaad!"

"Cockblocked by my own flesh and blood," he mutters as he sets me aside and stands to go see to her, making me giggle.

I know he's being silly. Gabby has always been, and will always be, his number one priority. And that's exactly how it should be.

I finish my wine and set the glass aside, then settle back again against the soft cushions and pillows of Carter's sofa. There's a throw blanket nearby, so I reach for it and toss it over me.

It's been a busy, eventful week. I never would have thought, even a week ago, that this is where I'd be tonight. Not here as an employee, but as something more. It's not awkward at all.

It feels . . . good.

So good, in fact, that my eyes are heavy, and I give in to the sleepiness.

"Shhh, don't wake her up."

I keep my eyes closed and listen to Carter and Gabby. They're close by. Maybe in the kitchen?

I take a deep breath and smell coffee and bacon.

Yep, they're in the kitchen.

"Why did she sleep over?" Gabby asks in a loud whisper.

"Because she fell asleep on the couch," Carter replies softly. "I'm serious, Gabs, don't wake her up. She's tired."

"I'm not gonna wake her up," Gabby says. "She looks comfy. I've never slept on that couch. Maybe I should try it."

"Are you going to keep talking?" Carter asks, making me smile. Of course she's going to keep talking. Talking is what Gabby does best.

The name *Gabby* fits her to a T.

"I'm not being loud," she says defensively, and I decide to put them both out of their misery.

"It's okay," I say and sit up, stretching my arms above my head. "I'm awake."

"Did I wake you?" Gabby asks. "'Cause if I did, Dad might strangle me."

"No, the delicious smell of bacon woke me," I say and pad into the kitchen. I stop by Gabby, who's sitting on a stool at the island, and kiss her forehead. "Your fever is a bit better this morning. Did you take more Tylenol?"

"Not yet," she says.

"I'll give you some," I offer. "After you eat. I see you have the oven mitts on."

"I can't stop scratching," she admits. "The mitts help, I guess. I look silly."

"And that's always fun," I reply with a wink. I walk around the island to see if I can help Carter cook breakfast.

"You guys aren't going to, like, kiss in front of me are you? I mean, I'm already sick."

"You mean like this?" I push up to my tiptoes and kiss Carter's cheek.

"Ew," Gabby says.

"Or like this?" Carter says, surprising me by wrapping his arms around my back and dipping me dramatically, the way they do in the movies. He kisses me soundly, and when we come back up, Gabby's face is one of pure mortification.

"Awww, how sweet," she says. "Don't ever do that in front of me again. I feel like I need to gouge my eyes out. Go to church. Take a bath."

"You're so dramatic, Gabs," Carter says with a laugh.

"You've just ruined my whole childhood with that disgusting display. Are you proud of yourself?"

"Ridiculously proud," Carter says. "And if one kiss ruined your whole childhood, I'm doing pretty well, I think."

"I might need a puppy to make up for it," Gabby says, making us all laugh.

Chapter Six

~Nora~

"That Quinn is one hunk of a hot man."

I sigh and roll my eyes as I march right into the employee lounge.

"Are you freaking kidding me?" I demand, and both Stephanie and Mary turn to gape at me with wide eyes. "You two are still gossiping about this stuff?"

"I mean, it was just an observation," Mary says, pushing her little chin in the air defiantly.

"You work in *HR*," I remind her. "You of all people know the rules around here and should behave a lot more professionally."

"Thank you," Stephanie mutters with a relieved sigh.

"Wait, what?" Mary demands, turning to Stephanie. "You *agree* with me."

"I smile and nod," Stephanie disagrees. "That's not the same. I'm just hoping you'll shut your trap. I know you work in HR, and I don't need you making my life hell, or finding a way to fire me, if I don't listen to your gossip. But frankly, I'm done."

Stephanie leaves the lounge, and I'm left with a seething Mary.

"I suppose you'll go tattle on me and get me fired," Mary says, glaring at me.

"I guess I just don't know where all this animosity is coming from," I say as I reach for a cup, filling it with hot water for my afternoon tea. "I don't recall ever having an issue with you in the past."

"You prance around here, in your perfect suits and your perfect shoes, like you're better than the rest of us."

I turn, gaping at her now.

"Excuse me?"

"You heard me. You and the other personal assistants of the partners, you're all just so snobby, it's disgusting."

"Number one," I begin and set my hot water aside before I throw it on her.

That would be frowned upon.

"I'm not a personal assistant"—*not technically*—"I'm an executive assistant. And I don't think I'm better than anyone. I'm doing my job. If you feel threatened by that, well, that's not my problem. That's on you."

"I do *not* feel threatened—"

"Number two," I interrupt. "If you have something to say about me, you can say it *to* me. I have some broad shoulders, I can take it. And yes, if you continue to act unprofessionally, I'll make the recommendation that you're fired."

"Well." Mary's nose wrinkles in anger and she stomps past me to the door, leaving without another word.

"Nice talking to you," I mutter as I finish making my tea, then walk to my desk. The Dickinson file is sitting on my desk, making my lips twitch and the horrible exchange with Mary melt away.

I open the file to find the expected note from Carter.

  N—

  Play hooky with me this afternoon.

                                                    —C

I sigh, shred his note, and reach for a blank piece of paper.

  C—

  We have too much work to do.

                                                    —N

I march into Carter's office, which is currently empty, and lay the file on his desk, then return to my own and get back to work. Fifteen minutes later, Carter walks past me, nods at me, and disappears in his office. Less than three minutes after that, he comes out with the file, sets it on the corner of my desk, and returns to his office.

I bite my lip and open the folder.

N—

I'm the boss, and I say you take the afternoon off.

—C

I want to laugh out loud, but I manage to hold it in as I write a note in response.

C—

How funny. You may be the boss here, but you're not the boss of our relationship.

—N

I walk it in to his desk. He's on the phone when I set the folder in his in-box. I wink and turn to walk back out.

Ten minutes later, Carter's whistling as he casually carries the file to me, places it in my hand this time, and without a word walks away.

This is getting ridiculous, but I admit, it's fun.

N—

Are you saying you don't *want to spend the day with me?*

—C

I frown as I shred that note and begin writing mine.

C—

Pack your bags, we're going on a guilt trip!

—N

I walk into Carter's office, and he takes the folder from me. But before I can walk out again, he says, "Wait."

He opens the folder and reads my words, then looks up at me with humor-filled blue eyes.

"Spend the day with me."

"Carter—"

"I'm not asking."

He's not moving from behind his desk, but he might as well be holding on to me with both hands, I feel so drawn to him.

"I can be ready to go in about thirty minutes," I finally say with a smile.

"Perfect."

He nods and I walk away, anxious to wrap up the few things

that need to be seen to right away, then take the rest of the day off with the man I'm quickly falling in love with.

"I CAN'T BELIEVE you haven't spent more time at the Met," Carter says an hour later as we stand in front of a painting of a woman in a black dress called *Madame X*.

"I've been a little busy," I say defensively. This museum is huge, there's no way we'll be able to see it all in an afternoon. "I work for a workaholic."

"You have weekends off," he reminds me and slips his hand into mine, giving it a squeeze. "Do you enjoy art?"

"Very much," I say with an enthusiastic nod. "Seeing the Louvre in Paris is on my bucket list."

"Really?"

I nod again and look up at him. I feel so short next to him, and I'm not a short woman. "Have you been?"

"No, but maybe I'll have to change that."

"I think everyone should see the *Mona Lisa* at least once in their lives," I say as we continue to casually stroll through the museum.

"They say she's small," Carter murmurs.

"I don't care if she's the size of a postcard." I stop to stare at a sculpture with no head. "Leonardo da Vinci touched it. It's incredible. I was an art minor in college."

"No kidding," Carter says in surprise. "That's cool, and something else I didn't know about you."

"I'm just one surprise after another," I reply with a laugh.

Carter tugs me gently against him and kisses my cheek. "You're making me crazy in these shoes."

I'm wearing the black heels with red bows. His favorite.

"Are the shoes the reason you were so adamant that we play hooky today?"

"Part of it," he admits without apology. "I'd take you home right now, but Gabby's there with Maggie."

"We're still looking at art."

His lips twitch as he gives my hand another squeeze. "I'm looking at the most beautiful work of art I've ever seen in my life."

Well, isn't he the charming one?

"No one's at my place," I remind us both, my breath coming a little faster now. "Why don't we go there?"

"I thought you'd never ask," he says with a laugh and leads me through the museum, and out the doors leading to the parking garage.

"How is Gabby feeling?" I ask once we're in his car. "Is she sick of being at home yet?"

"She's sassy as ever, so she's feeling better," he says. "She was vaccinated as a little one, so she's recovering quickly. She shouldn't be contagious by the weekend."

"I'm glad. Being sick sucks."

"Thank you for asking about her." Carter reaches for my hand and kisses my knuckles as he watches the crazy Manhattan traffic.

"I love Gabby, you know that."

"She loves you, too."

Once we arrive at my building, I show him where to park, thankful that my space is open, and I shoot the super a text, letting him know the car parked there is with me so he doesn't get towed, and lead Carter up to my place.

"How did you manage to score that parking anyway?" Carter asks. "In Manhattan, no less."

"The super likes me," I reply with a shrug. "And the person who owned my unit before me also used this spot, so he said I could have it as well, for a small monthly fee. And let me tell you, it's worth every penny."

He nods and follows me into the building.

My apartment is a quarter of the size of Carter's penthouse, but I love it. And I'm grateful that I changed the sheets on the bed yesterday.

We walk inside, shed our coats, and I immediately reach for Carter's hand and lead him directly to my bedroom.

Do not pass Go, do not collect $200.

I reach for him, unfastening the buttons on his expensive shirt, ready to finally have him naked and as turned on as I am right now, but he stills my hands.

"Slow," he says softly. "I haven't done this in a really long time, Nora."

"Me either," I admit with a grin. "And I want you."

He clenches his eyes shut, as if he's trying to keep himself under control. "Trust me, I want you more than I want my next breath."

"Awesome." I reach for his buttons again, but he swiftly spins me to the bed and has me flat on my back and my hands pinned above my head before I can blink. "You move really fast for such a big man."

"I was a sprinter in high school," he says and slides his tongue over my bottom lip. "We have to talk about a couple of things, sweetheart."

"I think we should just get down to business and talk later."

He laughs and drags his nose along my neck, sending every nerve ending in my body on high alert.

"Yes, more of that," I say breathlessly.

"Oh, I plan to do things to you that you didn't even know were possible," he says, making my core tighten in response. "But first, let's talk about safety."

"Always the attorney," I whisper. "I'm clean as a whistle."

"Of course you are," he says and nibbles my earlobe.

"No fair that you get to touch and kiss me but I don't get to do the same."

"Been a long-ass time," he reminds me. "If you touch me, I'll embarrass myself. Also, I'll keep you safe."

"What does that mean?"

"Birth control. I had a vasectomy five years ago."

I frown and stare up at him. "You did?"

He just nods. "We can talk about it more later, I just wanted to let you know that pregnancy isn't an issue."

"Awesome," I say with a grin. "Please tell me that's the end of the adult conversation so we can get down to the adult actions."

He laughs and buries his face in my neck again. "You smell so fucking good."

I had no idea Carter would be a dirty talker. In the past, sex was something to be had in the dark, with as little noise as possible.

And here we are, in broad daylight, making all kinds of sexy noises.

It's as if it's the first time for me all over again.

Carter's hands leave my wrists and slide down my arms, to begin pulling my clothes from my body. It takes him forever because as he uncovers flesh, he presses wet kisses, murmurs words of delight.

He's attentive and freaking sexy as hell.

"Carter, I need to feel you."

"You're going to feel *everything*," he whispers against my ear. He unfastens my skirt and wiggles it past my wide hips and down my legs. "Have I told you how much I fucking love your curves?"

"I don't think so."

"Well, I do. Your hips, your ass. Your breasts." He groans and tugs my nipple through my bra into his mouth, then pulls the lace down, uncovering both breasts. My hips surge up in invitation, and Carter slips right between them, still fully clothed. "God, you're so damn responsive."

"Are you going to get naked, or are you going to continue to torture me?"

He grins and plucks my nipple with his teeth.

"Patience, Nora."

"Not feeling particularly patient."

"I'm not going to hurry through this. So settle in and enjoy the ride."

I take a deep, soul cleansing breath and push my fingers into his thick, soft hair. With my eyes closed, I let myself give in to every sensation, every touch. His hands are freaking everywhere except the one place I long for them to be.

But it's not long before Carter moves down my body, leaving a trail of wet kisses in his wake. He pays extra special attention to my navel.

"That tickles."

"I had no idea you have an outie," he says, brushing the tip of his nose across the belly button in question.

"Now you do."

He presses a kiss there, then moves lower, and holy shit, this is exciting.

Carter Shaw is in my bed, doing the most delicious, unspeakable things to my body.

And I'm not sorry. Not sorry in the least.

I can't hold still. My hands are roaming through his hair, over his shoulders, and back through his hair again. My legs are moving up and down the sides of his body, practically begging to wrap around his waist.

"So damn sweet," he mutters before licking once, long and sure, up the slit of my core, making me cry out in joy.

Unlike my previous experiences, this man doesn't give me fifteen seconds of attention before climbing over me to take his own pleasure.

No, Carter seems to be camped out down there for the long haul, God love him.

"Carter," I moan, fisting my fingers in his hair now. "Oh God."

He moans, which only sends vibrations through me I've never felt before, and suddenly, without warning, an orgasm washes over me, completely consuming me and I can't hold it back.

I arch my back and cry out. And he doesn't lighten the pressure at all. He pushes a finger inside me and licks eagerly as I ride the waves of pleasure.

As I come back to Earth, Carter kisses my inner thighs, my hips, and up my body. He's cradling my head with one hand and shucking his pants with the other.

"Your shirt," I mutter.

"You want it gone?"

"Yes."

He pushes onto his knees and quickly discards his shirt, then covers me again and now I can touch his warm, smooth skin.

I turn my head and press a kiss to his bicep, and he seems to take that as an invitation to kiss my neck.

Holy mother of God, I'm not complaining.

"You're sure?" he whispers.

"I don't think I've ever been so sure of anything in my life."

His blue eyes are fixed on mine as he pulls his hips back, and as the tip of his cock finds my entrance, I close my eyes on a sigh.

"Eyes open," he says, and I comply. "I want to see what this does to you."

And he sinks inside me, all the way.

"Oh God," I moan and wrap my legs around his waist, keeping him seated fully inside me. "Carter."

"Yes," he murmurs and kisses my lips softly. He's cradling my head with both hands, his thumbs are brushing strands of hair off my cheeks. "God, you're incredible. So damn tight."

"Don't move yet."

He kisses my nose. He's so damn loving, it almost breaks my heart. So gentle. So sweet.

"You are incredible," he whispers against my lips before kissing me deeply. His tongue tickles the corner of my lips, and as I open my mouth to the kiss, he moves his hips, just rocking a bit to give us some friction. "So damn good."

I can't stop touching him as his movements become more hurried, chasing the orgasm building for both of us.

I bear down, and he tips his forehead against mine.

"Fuck, Nora."

"I don't think that's what this is," I whisper, making his lips tip up in a sweet smile, that dimple in his left cheek winking at me. I kiss him there and watch in fascination as he succumbs, falling over the edge and taking me with him.

"WHY DON'T YOU have Swiss?" Carter asks with a frown as he stares in my fridge. We've gone two rounds in the bedroom so far this afternoon, and we're both starving. He's decided we need grilled cheese sandwiches.

I think that's a brilliant idea.

"Well, I didn't know that you'd be craving Swiss on your grilled cheese after we had sex," I say with a saucy grin. "But you can bet your fine ass it's now on my grocery list."

"Sassy." He pulls me against him and kisses me long and slow. "I love it when you're sassy."

"That's good." My hand drifts up and down his naked spine. He's only wearing his slacks because I stole his button-down. "Because I'm sassy eighty-seven percent of the time."

"I'd bet it's more than that."

"Probably."

He kisses me again, and suddenly my front door is opened, and in comes Christopher. It's like Kramer on *Seinfeld*.

"I have to tell you—" He stops cold and stares in surprise at Carter. He hasn't loosened his hold on me. If anything, he's tightened it territorially. "Well. Sorry, I didn't know I was interrupting anything."

"Does he always barge in like this, darling?" Carter asks me, as if Chris isn't even here.

"Sometimes."

"Not anymore," Chris says. "Or you could just put a sock on the doorknob whenever the sexy lawyer's here."

I glare at Chris, who has yet to look away from Carter.

"Hey. Eyes over here, buddy. This one's taken."

"Right." Chris looks at me as Carter lets go and continues to build the grilled cheeses, turning his back to Chris.

Chris mouths, *OH MY GOD! HE'S SO FUCKING HOT!* And then makes obscene finger gestures, making it *very* difficult for me to not bust up laughing.

"So what did you have to tell me?" I ask him and shake my head, giving the signal for *STOP IT.*

"I have no idea."

"It was forty seconds ago," I say, frowning.

"Yeah, well, a lot's happened in forty seconds. And I should go because while you two don't seem to mind having a chat in basically nothing, I'm not supercomfortable."

"You're kidding."

Chris shakes his head and holds his hands up in surrender. "It's kinda weird feeling like the third wheel. So call me when lover boy here leaves, and then you can give me all the dirty details. Toodles!"

He waves, and just as dramatically as he entered, he leaves the apartment.

"Interesting friends you have, darling."

"You have no idea."

"Hungry?"

"Starved."

He passes me a fresh-off-the-griddle sandwich.

"I suppose this will do," I say with a wink. But before I can eat it, Carter slings me over his shoulder and stomps back to the bedroom. "Hey! My sandwich is gonna get cold."

"I'll make you a new one later."

Chapter Seven

~Carter~

I frown at the caller ID and answer the call on the third ring.

"Hello, Dad."

"Oh, hi there. I was expecting to leave a message." He clears his throat. "Your mother and I are having our estate planning reworked, and I need to mark down Gabby's birthday. I think it's March fifteenth, and your mother thinks it's March seventeenth."

I want to rip my hair out of my skull.

"You could have texted me."

"Well, this is just as easy, isn't it? So her birthdate is March fifteenth, yes?"

"Her birthday is February twentieth," I reply through gritted teeth. "Darcy's birthday was March fifteenth."

There's a pause. I'm sure he's calling himself an idiot.

He *is* an idiot.

Except, he's not. My father is a highly intelligent man. He's the best brain surgeon on the East Coast. He's well respected.

But he can't remember his granddaughter's birthday?

"It's good I called then," Dad says. No apology, of course. "We haven't seen either of you in quite some time, son. You and Gabby should come down for a visit."

Nora walks into my office and stops short when she sees I'm on the line. She moves to leave, but I wave her in and give her the signal for *I'll be off in just a minute*.

"We won't be coming for a visit," I reply to my father, watching Nora as she frowns and sinks into the chair in front of my desk. "Mom and I just went through this on her birthday. Which I remembered, of course. I don't know why you need Gabby's birthdate for your estate planning, as she's a minor."

"Well, we're setting up trusts and such. Making sure her college is paid for, of course."

"I can pay for my daughter's college." I rub my fingers deeply into my eye socket, trying to relieve the headache setting up residence there.

"We're her grandparents," Dad says. "Of course we want to help with her college expenses. And of course we will set up trusts for her, for both of you, in the event of our death."

"Do what you want," I say, ready to get the hell off the phone. "Is there anything else you need?"

"No." His voice is quiet now. "No, son, there's nothing else."

"Good-bye then."

I hang up and immediately stand to pace behind my chair.

"I take it that was your father?" Nora asks softly.

"The one and only."

"Did he suggest a visit?" she asks.

"He always does."

"Well, maybe you should visit. If he's asking to see you—"

"No." I turn to her, cutting her off. "No, I won't be going down there."

"I just think that since he invited—"

"I said no," I interrupt, my voice harder than I intended. "And it's really none of your business if I agree to visit them or not, Nora."

She looks down at her hands and I immediately feel like a dick, but I'm just so *frustrated*.

"Of course," she says and stands. "I was just popping my head in to tell you I'm leaving for the day. Have a great weekend."

"Wait."

But she doesn't stop walking. She marches right out the door, shutting it firmly behind her.

"God, Carter, you're a son of a bitch."

I hurry after Nora and see her putting her handbag on her shoulder, her face stoic. But her cheeks are flushed, and I can see the hurt in her gorgeous brown eyes.

"Nora, in my office, please."

"I was about to leave," she says, but I shake my head. There are benefits to being the boss.

"This will only take a minute."

She sighs but does as I ask and walks into my office. I close and lock the door behind her.

"I'm sorry, damn it. I didn't mean to sound like such a jerk."

"No, you're probably right," she says. "I have no right to make suggestions where your family's concerned. I'm just the assistant."

"Fuck that." I pull her in, wrap my arms around her, and hug her close. "You're not *just* anything, and you know it. Damn it, they get me so messed up in the head, I say and do things I regret. I'm sorry, darling."

"We're at work," she whispers, but she clings to me and presses her face to my chest, taking a deep breath. "This is against the rules."

"You've already clocked out," I remind her and kiss the top of her head. "And I couldn't bear to let you leave here mad at me."

"Hurt more than mad," she says.

"That's even worse." I tip her chin up and kiss her lips softly. "Come spend the evening with Gabby and me."

"I can't." She cups my cheek. "I'm going to see Christopher's show. I promised him weeks ago I'd be there for opening night."

I don't like it. Not because of Christopher, but because it's Friday night and I'd like to spend it with this amazing woman.

"Tomorrow then. We'll make a full day of it."

Nora smiles brightly. "I accept. I'll call you in the morning."

"Why don't you just come over in the morning? We'll decide what we want to do from there."

"Okay." She pushes up on her tiptoes to brush her lips against mine, and I deepen the kiss, pulling in even closer.

"I'll miss you tonight."

"It's just one night," she says before pulling away. "I'll come over as soon as I'm up and about tomorrow."

"See that you do."

"STRIKE!" GABBY YELLS and then does a silly happy dance right there on the lane. "I'm totally kicking both your butts."

"I'm totally letting you win," I say as she walks over and high-fives me. "Just to make you feel better."

"Whatever. You'd never let me win. You're too competitive."

"She's right," I say to Nora. "She's kicking our butts."

Gabby proudly shoves some lukewarm fries in her mouth and grins. "Can we have pizza?"

"You just had chicken fingers and fries," I say as Nora reaches for her ball and assumes the position on the lane. She takes four steps and lets go of the ball, which swerves to the left and only knocks down three pins.

"I'm making up for the days that I didn't have an appetite," Gabby replies. "I've been craving pizza all day."

"Yeah, well, you can wait just a little bit for that other food to settle."

"Want some of my nachos?" Nora offers Gabby, who nods and reaches for the chips and cheese.

"You can pick up that spare," I say to Nora and pat her on the butt, sure that Gabby's not watching.

"We'll see," Nora says as she retrieves her ball and bowls again, picking up all but one of the remaining pins. "Dang it! So close."

"You're getting better," Gabby says with encouragement. She looks expectantly at me. "Your turn, Daddy."

"I'm beginning to regret this little outing," I say. "Whose idea was bowling, anyway?"

"Uh, yours," Nora says with a laugh. "In fact, you were pretty adamant about bowling just two hours ago."

"I think this little girl's been bowling when I'm not home. She's way better than she was the last time we went."

"Some of us just have God-given talent," Gabby says. "Don't hate the player, hate the game."

"How old are you?" I demand as I fetch my ball and pay attention to the pins at the end of the lane. I take my stance and go through the motions, release the ball, and pump my fist when it *finally* knocks down all ten pins. "Yes!"

"Good one," Nora says and claps loudly, then hugs me when I return to my seat. I pull her in for a quick kiss.

"Hey. None of that," Gabby says with a scowl. "As in *none*. Ever."

"You'll live," I say as I reach over to ruffle her hair. "No more itching?"

"No, thank goodness. And I can go back to school on Monday, right?"

"I don't see why not. You're not contagious anymore."

"Good. I'm going to be so far behind, I don't even want to think about it."

"You're a smart girl, Gabs," I say with confidence. "You'll be okay."

"So those are the final scores," Nora says, pointing up at the screen. "Gabby cleaned our clocks at one forty-seven. Good job, girlie."

"Does this mean I get to choose what we do next?"

Nora and I share a glance.

"Depends on what you want to do," I say with a smile.

"Movies at home, curled up on the couch, and Nora makes the popcorn."

"Now, that we can do," Nora says as she unties her rental shoes. "Extra butter?"

"Of course," Gabby and I say together.

"ONE MORE."

I stare at my yawning daughter and shake my head no. "That's three in a row. You can't even keep your eyes open."

"Yes, I can," she insists, but her eyes drift closed despite herself. "We can watch another funny one."

"Tomorrow," Nora says. "There's still a whole day left in the weekend."

"I'll be right back," I murmur to Nora, then lift my daughter in my arms and carry her to the bedroom. She's way too old to be carried, but every once in a while I like to pretend she's still my baby.

"Why am I so sleepy?" Gabby asks into my shoulder.

"It's eleven," I remind her. "And you're still getting over the pox, my friend. You're bound to get tired easily."

"It sucks."

"I know." I kiss her cheek before lowering her to her bed. I tuck her in, and she's fast asleep before I turn off the light. "Good night, pumpkin."

Nora's not in the living room when I return. I round the corner to the kitchen, and sure enough, there she is, cleaning up from the movie popcorn and goodies, her hair twisted up into a messy knot on her head. She's in casual comfy clothes that she brought with her this morning because she didn't know what to expect out of today, and she wanted to be prepared.

That's my Nora, always prepared.

"How are you, darling?" I ask as I sit on a stool, watching her bustle around my kitchen. I know it sounds old-fashioned, but I like the way she looks in my kitchen. Hell, I just like the way she looks, no matter where we are.

"I'm fine," she says with a soft smile. "I had a good day."

"Me, too."

"I didn't know you were so good at bowling."

"I'm obviously not," I say with a laugh. "Gabby kicked my ass."

"She had fun, too. When you went to the bathroom between movies earlier, she asked me if things were going well. She said she asked you, but you're not good at giving details."

I stare at her, surprised. "What did you say?"

"I told her that we're doing well. That we enjoy spending time together. And I pretty much left it at that."

"It's all true," I say, rubbing my chin. "I guess she did ask me how you were the other day, but I thought she was just asking about *you*. I didn't realize she was fishing for inside information."

"She's curious," Nora says. "And that makes sense because it's been just the two of you for a long, long time. I'm just grateful that she likes me and isn't throwing a fit at the idea of you dating me."

"She's pretty levelheaded most of the time. I talked it over with her before our first official date. Not because I think I need her permission, but—"

"I get it," she says with a nod. "That was thoughtful of you. I should probably head home soon."

"Stay," I say immediately.

"Carter, Gabby's home. I don't know if that's a good idea."

"Gabby's not stupid," I reply and leave the stool to walk around the island and pull Nora against me. "She knows we're a couple, and trust me, if she had issues about it, she would voice them. And I'm not talking about the token kiss resistance she insists on voicing."

"I know." She smooths her hand down my chest, over my T-shirt. "I just don't want to be a bad example for her, you know? She's young, and impressionable."

"You're good for us," I murmur as I start to sway back and forth, feeling more at home with Nora in my arms than I have in what feels like forever. "We're not doing anything wrong, you know."

"Aside from having sex out of wedlock?" she reminds me. "I mean, I'm not superreligious or anything, but that's usually one that parents like to stick to."

"If she has questions, we'll answer them. Unless she asks questions, I'm not going to talk to my daughter about my sex life. I want you to stay. Gabby can see that we care about each other, and that what we have together is consensual and affectionate. She knows and trusts you. I don't see anything wrong with what we have."

"I don't either," she insists. "I just want to make sure we're all comfortable because a month ago I was your assistant. And now, I'm . . . well . . . I'm . . ."

"You're what?"

She looks up at me with tired brown eyes. "I don't know."

I lift her, not over my shoulder like last weekend when we were playing around, but rather cradling her to me as I carry her to my bedroom, which happens to be on the opposite end of the penthouse from Gabby's room, thank God.

I close and lock the door, and when we're both stretched out on the bed, I cup her jaw and lean in to press my lips to hers lightly.

"You're everything," I murmur. "If you want to call yourself my girlfriend, that's fine. Companion and lover work just as well."

"Carter," she whispers with tears in her eyes.

"If you think this is a fling, you're sorely mistaken."

She laughs and leans in to bite my chin. "Well, I was planning on taking another lover next weekend, since I've suddenly become so good at it."

I roll her under me, pinning her to my bed.

"Bullshit." I kiss the side of her mouth. "I dare you to try."

"Oh? And what will you do about it?"

I lean back and take her in, her blond hair spread over my blue sheets, her skin pale and brown eyes shining with lust and mischief.

God, I love her.

The thought of her ever not being here is one I can't entertain. It would break me.

"I'm going to ask you nicely," I say, rather than tell her I'd kill any man who would dare put a hand on her, "to save your body, your secrets, and the most vulnerable parts of you for me. Please."

"You say the most amazing things."

"Just what I feel." I kiss my way down her neck to her collarbone. Nora sighs and her body loosens under me, and I settle in to make love to the woman who's suddenly stolen my heart.

Chapter Eight

~Nora~

For the first time in ten years, I can honestly say I don't want to work today. Mondays have never bothered me. I enjoy my job and look forward to being in the office each day.

But after a weekend of laughter, relaxation, and the best sex of my damn life, I'm not ready for Monday.

The city is bustling this Monday morning. Winter has settled in, nestling New York in cold and snow. It's uncomfortable at best. I don't enjoy winter, never have. One day, I'd like to have a vacation place in the south, where I can escape a few weeks a year to soak up some sun.

But that's a dream for another day. It's back to work now, back to hiding my feelings for Carter and pretending that nothing is going on outside of the office.

I thought it would be an easy challenge.

I was wrong.

It's not easy to be with Carter, touching each other freely, and then turning it off like a faucet at work.

It's jarring. Uncomfortable.

It sucks.

But I still believe it's necessary, so here I am, wearing Carter's favorite shoes again, at his request of course, shoes that were slung over his broad shoulders just last night, walking into the building he's built with his brothers-in-law.

I'm early, since I spent the afternoon away from the office on Friday, also at Carter's request. I don't regret it. We need time away from here, where we can just be ourselves and learn each other.

But being gone on Friday means I have a to-do list the length of my leg to work on today.

Few people are here this early, so I go ahead and make a pot of coffee in the lounge, then carry a fresh cup to my desk and get settled. I've managed to work my way through a third of my list before the other assistants walk in, waving on their way to fetch their own coffee, and maybe some for their bosses as well.

It's just before eight when Carter walks in, nods at me, and walks into his office. I hate that I can't jump up, throw my arms around his neck, and kiss him. I can't even show that I'm happy to see him.

This whole no-frat policy sucks big-time.

A half hour after Carter arrived, he walks to my desk and passes me the Dickinson file, then returns to his office.

I bite my lip and open the file.

N—

> *Good morning, darling. You look beautiful today,*
> *but then you look beautiful every day. Just heard from*
> *Finn that London has a show opening this Friday*
> *night, and we're all invited, of course. I'd like to take*
> *you with us.*
>
> —*C*

I smile and shred the note, but before I can reply, my phone rings.

"This is Nora."

"Hey, it's Sienna. Do you have time to come to my office so I can bounce some thoughts off you?"

"Sure, I'm on my way."

"Thank you."

I shut down the computer, and grab my tablet, then walk down to Sienna's tidy office. She's sitting at her desk, her head in her hands.

"Is everything okay?" I ask.

"Is Mary in HR always a royal pain in the ass? I'm trying to hire an assistant here, and she's dragging her damn feet."

"Lately, yes, she is a pain in the ass . . . so you decided on one?"

"Two, actually, and that's why I called you. I need to make a final decision this morning, and these two candidates are both more than qualified. I liked them both. So I thought I could use a second set of eyes and ears."

"Sure, who did you narrow it down to?"

She passes me the two résumés, and I remember them both from last week's interviews.

"Good choices," I say with a nod. "I liked them both, too."

"Not helping. Did you like one of them better?"

I sigh, thinking it over. "Alice seemed more go-gettery, you know? But Victoria was calm and seemed more laid back."

"Yeah," Sienna says. "I'm leaning toward Victoria, now that you say that. I need someone willing to go with the flow."

"I think she'd be a good choice."

Sienna nods and then tilts her head as she examines my face. "Is everything okay with you?"

"Sure, why?"

"You look . . . concerned."

I sigh. I want to confide in her. I *need* to. So I stand and close her office door, then return to my seat.

"Must be good," she says.

"Carter invited me to go to London's show on Friday, and I don't have anything to wear."

Sienna frowns. "Wait. Are you two dating?"

"You mean Quinn hasn't said anything to you?"

"Noooo," she says slowly. "What's going on?"

"Well, I'm dating Carter. I guess that's what you'd say."

"Are you going out on dates?"

"Yes."

"Then yes, you're dating." Sienna grins. "And good for both of you."

"Thanks. But it's complicated, and please don't say anything here at work because we have to pretend that we're *not* dating when we're here."

"No-frat policy," she says with a nod. "I get it. I fell in love with Quinn when we were working together."

"That's right." I scoot to the edge of my seat. I've found a kindred spirit. "Didn't you feel guilty?"

"Oh yeah," she says with a nod. "He was opposing counsel."

"Yikes."

"You're not kidding. But we were *so* attracted to each other, you know?"

"Yeah." I swallow and nod slowly. "I know. It's new, but I know."

"Quinn just told me about the show on Friday, and I don't have anything to wear either. Let me call London right now and we'll have a girls' shopping spree."

"Oh, you don't have to—"

"Hold on," she interrupts and lifts her phone, dials a number and waits for an answer. "Hey girl, I'm gonna put you on speaker. Nora's with me."

She pushes a button.

"There."

"Hi, Nora," London says cheerfully through the phone. "What's up, ladies?"

"First, congrats on the show opening this Friday," Sienna says.

"Oh! Thanks. I'm so sorry for the late notice. I thought I'd already told the guys about opening night, and this morning Finn said that I hadn't."

"It's totally okay, but we don't have anything to wear," Sienna replies. "So we need a girls' evening of shopping. When are you free?"

"Tonight," London says. "In fact, tonight's my *only* night. Starting tomorrow we have evening dress rehearsals."

"Perfect," Sienna says. "Nora? Does tonight work?"

"Sure," I reply. "Sounds like fun."

"Oh, it's going to be better than fun," London says with a laugh. "It's *shopping*. And I need a girls' night STAT. YAY! Thanks for calling."

"Okay, Nora and I will leave the office at six and pick you up," Sienna says, making notes. "Will you be ready?"

"I'm more than ready," London assures us. "My credit card is already weeping with joy."

I feel my eyes go wide. What did I just get myself into?

"Oh my God, this is good," Sienna says as she bites into a soft pretzel. We didn't want to stop for dinner, so we grabbed something quick, planning to get a real meal when we're finished spending all the money in the world.

Well, that's their plan. I, however, don't plan to spend too much.

That plan is thwarted, however, two hours and four heavy shopping bags later.

"I bought *two* new pairs of shoes," I mutter in shock. "Three dresses and a suit."

"And don't forget that new Chanel eye shadow," London reminds me. "It's going to be *killer* with your brown eyes."

My credit card is weeping in agony, and you know what? I'm not sorry. Not sorry in the least.

I've known both these women since they found their men, and from a professional aspect, I like them very much.

But spending time with them as friends? It might be the best time I've ever had.

I don't have many female friends. Not because I don't get along well with women, but because I work 90 percent of the time. And when I don't work, I still help Carter out. Christopher befriended *me*.

And today has shown me that friendship is something I've been craving. Girl talk. Laughter. Shopping for ridiculously expensive shoes just because they're pretty.

"Are you okay?" Sienna asks me. "London, I think she's shell-shocked."

"I know I am," I admit with a laugh. "But in a great way. I don't think I've ever shopped like this before."

"We need to make this a regular thing," London says as she shifts her own bags from one hand to two. "And it's not over yet. What do you girls say instead of going out for dinner, we grab takeout and go back to Nora's place to look at our goodies?"

"Why my apartment?" I ask in surprise.

"No boys there," Sienna reminds me. "Girl talk is better when no boys are involved."

"That's why it's called girl talk," London adds with a wink. "What do you think?"

"I'm game," I agree, excited to spend more time with them both. I see why Quinn and Finn are so in love with these girls. They're fun and smart. Easy to be with.

I'm happy for all four of them all over again.

"HOLY SHIT," SIENNA says, a dirty martini with three olives in her hand, as she stares at my wall of shoes. "*Shoes.*"

"I have a thing for them," I say and sip my own martini. "It's really more of an obsession."

"I never used to care about shoes," Sienna says as she continues to look. "I had the same dull pair that I wore with *everything.*"

"What happened?"

"Quinn," she says simply. "He bought me a pair of Louboutins, and there was no going back."

"I splurge on my shoes," I admit. "I like the designer brands. And I wear them, so I don't feel like it's a waste."

"Let me try them on." Sienna spins to me, excitement dancing in her eyes. "Please?"

"You want to try on my . . . shoes?"

"You might as well let her," London says as she peruses my suits. "She'll just badger you until you let her."

"I will not," Sienna says with a dignified sniff. "Okay, I will. *Pleeeease?*"

"Sure." I laugh and sit on my bed, sip my drink, and dig into the bags of treasures I bought today. "I forgot about this necklace."

It's a silver chain with a simple butterfly pendant. It has teal wings.

"Look!" Sienna walks out of the closet in a pair of Jimmy Choo stilettos. They're covered in crystals. "We're the same size!"

"Uh-oh," London says with a laugh. "She may never leave."

"Quinn will come looking for me sooner or later."

Sienna disappears back into the closet, and London pours us all another martini.

"So you and Carter," she says with a grin. "Spill it."

"Spill what?"

"The sex," Sienna calls out from the closet. "Tell us about the sex."

I feel my cheeks flush as I take another sip of my drink and reach for a box of brand-new heels. "I don't think it's appropriate to talk about our sex life."

"Why?" London asks. "You're banging him, aren't you?"

"Well, yeah, but—"

"No buts," London says with a shake of the head. "I mean, unless you enjoy that sort of thing."

This drink is going straight to my head. I snort, and Sienna lets out a loud laugh in the closet. "No, I don't think I do."

"Actually, I want you to start from the beginning," Sienna says, carrying out an armful of shoes to try on. "How did this come about?"

And so, for the next twenty minutes, I tell them about my history with Carter, working for him forever, and how things started to change.

"The ol' stuck-at-the-office trick," Sienna says with a knowing nod after I tell them about being stuck in the storm. "Works every time."

"I don't think Carter could control a blizzard." I frown into my empty martini glass, and London fills it again from the shaker she's had a constant vodka supply in.

"And the sex is good?" London asks softly. They're both glassy-eyed, red-cheeked, and now that every shoe in my closet has been tried on and in a heaping pile on my bedroom floor, we're just lounging and gossiping about my love life.

London and I are on the bed, and Sienna is sitting on the floor, her back braced against my dresser.

"It's the best I've ever had," I confide softly. "So different from when I was married."

"Hold up," London says. "You were *married*?"

"For about six years," I say with a nod. "Richard and I met in college. We were both from small towns in Ohio, and we were just so young."

I set my half-empty glass aside.

"What happened?" Sienna asks.

"There's a list of things. He didn't like the number of hours I put in for Carter. He said I was never home, and that's why he was forced to find someone else to have sex with."

"Whoa," London says, sitting up straight. "What in the actual hell?"

"I didn't mean to say that. I'm a little drunk."

"I'm a lot drunk," Sienna says with a grin. "Keep talking."

"My marriage failing was my fault." I shrug. "I didn't pay him enough attention."

"He was a jealous asshole," London says. "You had a demanding career. There's no crime in that."

"Yeah, he didn't like it. He also hated that I earned more money than him."

"What's up with these insecure idiots who can't deal with a successful woman?" Sienna demands the room at large. "I mean, we're well into the twenty-first century."

"You're so much better off without him," London agrees.

"I know. However, my parents don't think so. I should be getting a call any day from my mother, reminding me to come back to Ohio to grovel for Richard to take me back."

"Who wants to be married to someone named *Richard*?" Sienna asks, scrunching up her nose. "It's so formal. Did you call him Rick?"

"Or Dick?" London adds with a smirk.

"Definitely no nicknames allowed," I say, shaking my head. "I once called him Rick, and he said, *my name is Richard.*"

"Ugh," Sienna says. "So I bet the sex was all formal, too."

"And about twice a year," I agree. "Carter can't keep his hands off me."

"That's how it should be," London says. "The man you're with should want to be intimate with you. He should cherish you. He should *not* ever want to humiliate you or make you feel bad for being successful at what you do."

"Why would your parents want you to stay with someone like that?" Sienna asks.

"Because divorce is a big no-no."

"Well, I'm glad you have us," London says and Sienna nods in agreement. "We think you're amazing, and divorcing Rick the Dick was the best thing ever, second only to having sex with Carter."

"Cheers to that." I clink my glass to theirs and sigh in happiness. "Thanks for being so nice to me."

"We're in this together," Sienna says. "Only we know what it's like to be with these men. They're not easy."

"But they're worth it," London says.

OH GOD. MY head. My alarm is trying to kill me. I shut it off and roll over, coming face-to-face with a snoring London.

Last night comes rushing back to me, and I can't help but smile, despite the jackhammer pounding in my temporal lobe.

I had the *best* time. We shopped. Sienna tried on my shoes. We talked about sex and shoes and *everything*.

And then we fell asleep.

I frown, remembering that Sienna should be here somewhere, and shuffle out to the kitchen. Sienna's sleeping soundly
on my couch, curled up in two of my throw blankets.

I'm going to be late for work today. Another first.

I find my cell in my purse and discover five texts from Carter.
With a wince, I open them, but he's not mad.

> I hope you're having a fun time with Si and London.
>
> Did you happen to have dinner?
>
> Please call me when you get home.
>
> Blink twice if you haven't been abducted by a serial
> killer.
>
> Did you dump me and I wasn't aware?

I grin and shoot him a text in return.

> Sorry! My phone was in my bag. I had a blast last night.
> In fact, I'm a smidge hungover and will be late coming
> into the office today.

I send the text and turn to see Sienna sitting on the couch,
wiping the sleep from her eyes. "Damn, my head."

"I'll get you some Advil. I need some myself." I pull the
bottle out of the cabinet, just as London walks out of the bedroom. Her hair is a curtain over her face.

"Why is it so bright in here?"

"Because we might have had a bit too much fun last night,"

Sienna says, gratefully accepting the pills and the bottle of water I pass her. "Thanks."

"I need some of that," London says. "And coffee. All the coffee in all the land."

My phone buzzes with a text from Carter.

> Hungover? What the hell happened last night?

I show Sienna my phone and she laughs, then shows it to London.

"I guess we'd all better let the guys know we're alive."

London and Sienna reach for their phones and I reply to Carter.

> I made some new friends. Sienna tried on my shoes and we drank all the vodka in Manhattan. I'll be there by ten.

"I have rehearsal in an hour," London says with a groan.

"I don't have to be to the office until noon," Sienna says.

"I'm already late," I add and we all grin at one another. "When are we doing it again?"

Chapter Nine

~Carter~

could have gone with Grandma tonight, so you could pick Nora up by yourself and have a gross kissing sesh in the limo."

I stare down at my daughter, who's all dolled up in an adorable blue dress, with curled hair and just a hint of mascara on her lashes, not that I think she needs it, but she begged.

And she's been such a trooper lately, I couldn't turn her down.

I did, however, say no to the *winged eyeliner*. Whatever the hell that is.

"I want you with me," I reply mildly. "Are you excited for tonight?"

"I always love to go to London's shows," she replies. "Maybe I want to be an actress when I get older."

"Well, your aunt London can give you lots of pointers."

The driver parks in front of Nora's building.

"I'll wait here," Gabby says.

"No way, you're coming with me. *We're* picking her up."

Gabby doesn't roll her eyes. She doesn't frown. A smile slides over her face and she hurries out of the car with me.

I don't know why she thinks that I don't want to include her in things with Nora and me. We love having her with us.

I'll have to explore this more later.

We take the elevator up to Nora's floor and ring her doorbell. Seconds later, she opens the door, and it's all I can do to keep my jaw off the floor.

"Whoa," Gabby says. "You're *so pretty*!"

"Thanks." Nora flushes and glances down at her black gown. It flows to just below the knee, showing off her beautiful calves and red heels. The dress is strapless, but she has a faux fur wrap draped over her shoulders. She's painted her lips red and pulled her hair up into an intricate knot at the back of her head.

"I don't have the words," I murmur and lean in to press a kiss to her cheek. "You're absolutely stunning."

"You're both good for my ego," she says with a little laugh and reaches for her red clutch. "And you also look fantastic. Both of you. Gabby, I love your shoes."

My daughter preens and rocks back on her heels, showing off her black, sparkly shoes that have a small heel on them. She's trying to grow up so fast, but I'm holding strong on keeping her in clothes appropriate for her age.

"Thanks," Gabby says. "I wanted higher heels, but Dad wouldn't let me."

"They'll just make you miserable," Nora says with a wink. "You made a wise decision."

"I like the sparkles," Gabby agrees. "Dad got us a limo."

"Fancy," Nora says. "Should we go then?"

I gesture for the ladies to lead the way to the elevator, making sure Nora's door is locked up tight behind us.

I reach for Nora's hand and link her fingers with mine. "You take my breath away," I whisper into her ear.

The doors open before Nora can reply, and Gabby leads us out to the limo, where the driver is waiting to open the door for us.

"Miss," he says with a happy nod to Gabby as he opens the door and then turns to Nora. "Welcome aboard, madam. There are refreshments for you, but the drive won't take long."

"Thank you," Nora says with a smile as she climbs inside. I sit next to her, with Gabby facing us. "Wow, this *is* fancy."

"Have you ridden in a limo before?" Gabby asks her.

"Once, for prom my senior year of high school," Nora replies. "But it wasn't this nice. How about you?"

"Yeah," Gabby says with a nod. "We take them a lot to things like this, and sometimes to and from the airport."

"Of course," Nora says. I hear a twinge of nerves in her voice.

"Having a car service on hand is helpful when you travel as much as Maggie does," I explain. "And she loves to take Gabby on vacation with her."

"We're going to Hawaii for spring break," Gabby says. "Hawaii is our favorite place."

"Well, that sounds like a ton of fun. I've never been there, so you'll have to tell me everything about it. And show me pictures."

"Where do you like to travel?" Gabby asks.

"I haven't done much traveling," Nora admits. "I went from being a struggling college student to moving to New York. And then I started working for your dad, and I just haven't had a lot of time to get away."

Because my wife died, and I leaned on Nora for literally everything, including finding me the penthouse and helping me with Gabby.

I've demanded a lot from her over the years.

I owe her a lot.

"Maybe when Gabby and Maggie go to Hawaii, you and I can sneak away somewhere," I suggest.

"That would be lovely."

The limo stops at the curb in front of the theater, and the driver opens the door for us, taking both Gabby's and Nora's hands to help them out of the car.

"Thank you," I say. "We'll need a ride after the show to dinner, and then home later."

"I have the itinerary, Mr. Shaw. You just enjoy your evening."

I nod and escort my girls into the building. London always reserves seats for us in our own section of the theater, where we can see and hear everything clearly.

We have the best seats in the house.

"You're here," Sienna says with delight and hugs Nora close, surprising me. I know they're friendly, but I didn't realize they'd become close so quickly. "And that dress is a knockout."

"Thanks," Nora replies, hugging her back. "But Gabby's stealing the whole show with her amazing ensemble."

Gabby giggles and does a little curtsy. "Thank you, thank you."

"She's humble as well," I say dryly, accepting a kiss on the cheek from Maggie. "You've met Nora, Maggie."

"Of course I have," Maggie says, taking Nora's hand in hers and giving her a hug. "It's so good to see you, dear. And, if I might say, it's about time."

Maggie pulls away and winks at both Nora and me. I couldn't have asked for a better reception for either of us. I've never brought a woman to a family function before because there was never a woman to bring, but I admit, I was nervous about it.

Darcy was Maggie's daughter. I didn't know how a new woman in my life would be received.

I can see now that I didn't need to worry.

"Welcome, everyone," London says with a grin. She usually comes out to say hello before the first show. It's become tradition. "I'm so happy you're all here."

"There's nowhere else we'd be, honey," Maggie says. "You just go out there and knock 'em on their ass."

"Mom," Quinn says with a laugh.

"What? Our girl is the best there is."

"Break a leg, London," Gabby says gleefully. "You're gonna rock it."

"I love you all." London's fighting tears as Finn leans in to whisper in her ear. She nods and smiles up at him, then waves at us all and returns backstage.

"I didn't think I'd be this nervous for her," Nora says, wringing her hands. "Are you guys ever nervous for her?"

"Every time," Sienna says, blowing out a long breath. "But we don't need to be. She's amazing."

The lights flicker, signaling that it's showtime.

"Here we go," I say and take Nora's hand in mine.

"I'M SO HUNGRY," Gabby says once the show is over and we're standing to stretch our legs and wait for London to finish up backstage.

"We're going out for a late dinner," Quinn tells her. "You do look extra pretty tonight, you know."

"Thanks," Gabby says. "Can I have steak?"

"You can have anything you want," London says as she joins us. "We're celebrating!"

"You were absolutely marvelous!"

Everyone takes turns hugging London and congratulating her on a job well done. She just spent two hours singing, dancing, and acting, and I don't know how she can possibly look like she's energized enough to do it all over again, but she does.

As we're walking out of the theater and onto the sidewalk to the limo, Nora stiffens next to me.

"What is it?"

She looks up at me with worried brown eyes. "Nothing."

We climb into the limo, alone this time because Gabby wanted to ride with London and ask a million questions.

"Talk to me, darling."

"Mary from the office was there," she says, shaking her head. "I didn't know that any employees would be there."

"We always give out a few pairs of tickets, in a random draw. It'll be okay."

"She *saw* us," Nora insists. "And she's already a huge pain in the ass at work. If I'd known she would be there, I wouldn't have come."

"Hey." I take her hand in mine and kiss her palm, then place it over my heart. "It's going to be fine. I brought you as my guest, and that's *my* business. If she says anything to you, you send her to me."

"You're right." Nora nods and leans her head on my shoulder. "It'll be fine."

But she's still stiff next to me. This bothered her.

I raise the privacy glass and then scoop Nora onto my lap and cup her cheek, staring up into her sweet face.

"You make me crazy. You know that, right? Are these new shoes?"

"They're new," she confirms and kisses my forehead. "I think we'll be at the restaurant soon."

Without looking away from her, I press the intercom button. "Circle the block three times, please."

"Yes, sir."

"There." I brush my lips over hers. "That gives me a few minutes to taste you."

"Aren't you hungry?"

"Starving. For you. It's been a few days."

"I'm aware," she says with a grin, finally loosening up. "I'm glad you like my shoes."

"I can't wait to get you out of this stunning dress and into my bed, in nothing *but* these shoes."

"I had no idea you had such a fetish when it came to footwear," she says and then sighs when I snake my hand up under the hem of her dress and find her not wearing any panties.

"I didn't. Until you." I let my fingers slide over the lips of her swollen pussy. "Is this all for me?"

"You're the only one here."

"Such a smart mouth." I bite her lower lip and then soothe it with my tongue. "I might spank you for that later."

"God, I hope so."

"You like it rough, darling?"

"If you're the one giving it to me, yes."

"I'm the *only* one, Nora."

She grabs my face in both hands and kisses me until my head is spinning.

"The car stopped," she murmurs against my lips.

"We'll pick this up later," I assure her, and set her on the seat so she can straighten her dress and check her lipstick.

"Your lips are red."

I pull my handkerchief out of my jacket pocket and wipe my lips.

"It might be your color."

"Two swats," I say, making her laugh. "Now, let's feed you so I can make you hungry again later."

"You say the sweetest things."

The door opens, and Nora exits the car. I follow her inside the restaurant where the others are already seated at a table in a private room.

"Sit by me," Gabby says to Nora.

"What about me?"

"You can sit by Nora," Gabby replies primly.

"I see where I rate." I laugh as I sit next to Nora and we spend the next hour and a half talking about London's show, eating delicious food, and generally enjoying one another.

I love the Cavanaugh family more than I can measure. I'm grateful for them every day, but it's nights like this one, when we're all together, that I'm reminded how lucky I really am.

They didn't have to continue including me after Darcy died, but they did.

I don't know how I can ever repay that.

"I think Gabby and I are getting tired," Maggie says with a happy sigh. "What a wonderful evening it was, though. There's nothing better than having my family all together."

"Can I spend the weekend with you, Grandma?" Gabby asks her.

"Of course you can. We'll plan our trip." Maggie winks at me. "Shall we go then?"

"Yeah. I need to get my makeup off and moisturize my face. I'm not getting any younger," Gabby says.

"Where do you get this stuff?" I ask.

"YouTube." She shrugs and then works her way around the table, hugging everyone good-bye. When she gets back to me, she wraps her arms around my shoulders. "I love you, Daddy."

"I love you more, pumpkin."

Saying *I love you* took some getting used to. My parents just didn't throw those words around, and it wasn't a habit for me. Sometimes, it still isn't. But man, I love my daughter.

"See you on Sunday," Gabby says and then follows Maggie out to their limo.

"She's such a sweet girl," London says after they walk out. "I'm glad she's doing better."

When London first met my daughter more than a year ago, Gabby was struggling. Her attitude was horrible, and in a desperate move, I sent Gabby to stay with Finn at his beach house for a few weeks in the summer. London also owns a house on Martha's Vineyard, and that's how she met Finn.

"It seems the worst of it is over."

"Until she hits sixteen," Quinn says cheerfully. "That will be fun."

"I'll just send her to live with you," I offer and laugh when Quinn's face sobers.

"I'll end up in jail for killing some punk trying to get in her pants."

"We'll all be in jail for that," Finn says.

"I'll defend you all and get you off," Sienna offers, making us laugh. "I don't even want to know what kind of a delinquent you were when you were sixteen."

"No," Quinn agrees and kisses her cheek. "You don't want to know."

I glance at Nora, who's smiling and watching the conversation around us. She's had only one cocktail, so her cheeks are rosy, but her eyes are clear.

"What are you thinking?" I ask her, and the others quiet to listen to her answer.

"That you're all wonderful," she immediately says and then presses her lips together.

"Go on," Finn says.

"I've known you guys for a long time," she begins and watches her fingers as she fiddles with the stem on her glass. "And I've respected you. Was fond of you. You're fair and kind to your employees, and working for you is something I've always been proud of."

"You're giving them big heads," London warns her.

"I've been around for a lot," she continues and looks up at us. "But it occurs to me that I've never socialized with you until tonight. Not as a family, outside of work events."

"We're crazy," Quinn says, but Nora shakes her head.

"No, you're family..I never had this. I'm an only child, and my parents and I have a different . . . philosophy. So gatherings like this are new to me."

"And what do you think?" Finn asks, watching her closely. "Are you ready to run yet?"

Nora smiles at him and shakes her head. "Nah. I don't want to run. And thanks for including me tonight. I had a great time."

I reach for her hand and kiss her palm. "You're always welcome here."

"Especially if I can keep trying on your shoes," Sienna agrees.

"You've created a monster," Quinn says playfully. "An expensive one at that."

"You started it," Nora replies and points at him from across the table. "And you can afford it."

"I *really* like you," London says. "Like, a lot."

"I like you, too." Nora laughs. "I feel like you're my tribe. But not in a creepy, stalker way."

"You're absolutely part of our tribe," Sienna says. "You're our kind of people."

Nora blushes, and I want to whisk her away, to make her blush all over her sexy body.

And why shouldn't I? We're childless for the next forty-eight hours, and I plan to take advantage of every single one of those hours.

"Let's go," I say, standing from my seat.

"What's your hurry?" Finn asks with a cocky grin.

"An empty house and a sexy woman," I reply. "You should take advantage of the same."

"Oh, I plan to," Finn says.

Nora gathers her things, and after we say our good-byes, I lead her out to the limo.

"My place or yours?" I ask her.

"I don't care as long as you're naked in about thirty seconds after we hit the front door."

My mouth drops as I watch her send me a sassy wink and lower herself into the limo. I mentally calculate where we are in relation to our homes and then look at the driver.

"My place. STAT."

"On it, sir."

Chapter Ten

~Nora~

I don't think I've ever been this turned on in my freaking life. If I don't get him naked in about four seconds, I might spontaneously combust.

And that's not sexy.

I can't even touch him in the elevator. I glance over at him and grin. Carter's watching the numbers climb with impatience, rubbing his hands together and bouncing on the balls of his feet like he's about to run a marathon.

"Impatient?" I ask. He turns those hot blue eyes down to me and I want to climb him like a tree.

Before he can reply, the elevator reaches the penthouse level. We hurry to the front door, and once he's unlocked the door, we rush inside, and I'm immediately pinned to the closed door, Carter's mouth on mine, his hands tangled in my hair.

"Too many pins," he mutters against my lips and begins

gently plucking the hairpins from my hair and dropping them onto the floor. "I fucking love your hair."

"My *hair*?" I laugh and tug his jacket down his arms, tossing it aside. My fingers can't open the buttons on his shirt fast enough.

"Your hair." He presses a kiss to my cheek. "Your eyes." Kisses my chin. "Your tits."

Jesus, he's going to kill me.

Finally, the last pin is pulled free and my hair spills over his hands as I'm trying to tug his tie free.

"You're wearing way more clothes than me," I mumble before Carter spins us around and boosts me onto the kitchen counter, where he continues to plunder my mouth, his hands roaming freely over my hyperaware flesh. "Strip."

"Yes, ma'am."

I watch with humor and awe as he sheds the rest of his clothes, then stands before me, fully aroused, and naked as the day he was born.

"Damn, Carter."

Muscles for days. The man has *muscles for days*. When does he find time to work out, that's what I want to know. Because a man with abs like that? He works out.

"You look at me like that for much longer, and I'll make a fool of myself."

Without replying, I hop off the counter and squat in front of him, immediately taking the head of his impressive cock in my mouth. Carter's hands dive into my hair as the breath hisses between his clenched teeth.

"Fucking hell, Nora."

I worship him, licking and sucking the length of him. With one hand working him, the other is everywhere, from his balls to his inner thighs, and deep female satisfaction takes root when I feel him break out in goose bumps.

I'm still in my dress and heels, and nothing else. Who knew that not wearing underwear kept you in a constant state of arousal?

Well, I know now.

"Stop," he mutters, but he doesn't lose his hold on my hair. "I don't want to come yet."

I keep going, reveling at how powerful I feel right now, but before I can make him finish, he grips my shoulders and pulls me up to my feet.

"I don't want to come yet," he repeats and kisses me long and hard, boosting me back onto the kitchen counter. "And you're way overdressed for this."

His hand glides over the skin of my inner thigh, and I spread my legs in invitation to keep exploring. He doesn't disappoint.

When he reaches my drenched core, his hot eyes spring to mine.

"This is a surprise."

"Oh yeah." I sigh when one finger pushes inside me the way he did in the limo earlier. "I've decided to go without underwear from now on."

"You'll kill me," he mutters as he presses his lips to my neck and nibbles lazily. He's suddenly gone from 120 mph to idle, and it's a jolt to my system. His fingers are taking a slow journey through my folds, over my swollen skin, and back inside where I'm slick and ready for him. "You're absolutely amazing."

"I want you," I say. It's not a whisper or a whimper. It's a declaration, here and now, of what I want.

"Do you," he says and kisses my hand, then presses it over his heart, the way he did earlier.

It's the kind of move that could bring a woman to her knees.

If I were on my feet.

Which I'm not.

"Carter." I take his face in my hands and gaze into his ocean-blue eyes.

I love you.

I want to say the words. I *long* to say them.

But not like this, not when we're making love.

"What do you need, Nora?"

"You." I nip his lower lip. "Right now."

"Bossy little thing, aren't you?" He grins, and the next thing I know, he's tossed me over his shoulder and is carrying me fireman style to the bedroom. He slaps my ass, leaving a zing on my cheek in its wake.

"Hey!"

"You said you liked the rough stuff."

I bite my lip in giddy anticipation.

"I didn't realize that included carrying me like a caveman."

He tosses me onto the bed, turns me over, and slaps my ass again, then presses his lips over the sting.

"Let me show you exactly what it entails, darling."

"WAKE UP, NORA."

I bury my face deeper into the pillow.

"I need you to wake up."

"Hmph." I turn my head and open one eye. "It's still dark."

"It's four," he says calmly.

"In the morning?" I scowl and sit up now. "Oh, did you want to—"

"I always want to." He kisses me softly, cupping my cheek. But before I sink into him properly, he backs away. "But I can't get sidetracked right now. We have to go."

"Are we being evacuated? Am I still dreaming?"

He grins, showing me that dimple in his left cheek. "I'm taking you somewhere. The plane's ready."

"*The* plane? As in, the company plane?"

"That's the one."

"I haven't packed anything. I don't—"

He pulls me to him and quiets me by kissing me once more. "You don't need anything. I have it all taken care of. Your only job is to enjoy yourself."

"I didn't order the plane for you."

"I have others who can do that for me, you know."

I narrow my eyes at him, but don't argue. I'm too excited to see where we're going.

HE UNLOCKS THE door of the condo on the top floor and ushers me inside. It smells of lemon, indicative of recently being scrubbed clean.

"Florida," I say for the third time, wondering if he's able to read minds. Wasn't I just thinking the other day that I'd like to go to Florida in the winter? "You rented us a condo for the weekend?"

"I own it," he says absently and leads me through the large unit, showing me bedrooms and bathrooms, the kitchen and living space, and finally out onto a balcony with a view of the surf hitting golden sand. There are little walking bridges that rise over sand dunes and down to the surf below.

"How did I not know that you own this condo?"

"The building, actually," he says, stunning me. I stare at him, my jaw hanging open, and he chuckles.

"I know just about everything there is to know about you, and I didn't know this."

"You don't know everything," he insists and kisses the palm of my hand, then rests it over his heart, which is becoming a habit. "You know what I've shown you, and I don't mean that to sound controlling or like I'm an asshole. But Nora, up until recently you were my assistant, and you took care of affairs that I assigned to you."

I'm watching the struggle on his handsome face, not a little flummoxed. I was so sure I knew him so well, and yet, he seems to surprise me at every turn.

"How long have you owned this?"

"Do you remember about six months ago when I had to come to Florida for a few days?"

"When your grandfather died," I say, nodding. I'd met

Carter's paternal grandparents a couple of times when they visited New York. They are the only family I've ever met of Carter's.

"That's the time," he confirms. "I inherited the building from him. They used to own a huge house on the golf course nearby, but as they aged, it became too much for him to keep up with."

"So he bought an entire building?" I ask, stunned. "I didn't know they were that wealthy."

"Granddad was a brilliant surgeon and earned more money from his breakthroughs in brain surgery than he could ever spend. But he was humble with it," Carter says with a smile. "He wasn't really a boastful man. But he and Grandma lived comfortably. This building was really an investment for him. He liked to dabble in real estate after retirement."

"Some people never fully retire," I murmur, watching the waves pound into the sand. "And this is a lovely place to spend some time."

"Let me go brew you some coffee," Carter says before kissing my cheek. "It's early yet."

"Someone pulled me from bed in the wee hours of the morning," I remind him with a laugh.

"I wanted to get here as soon as possible, so we could spend as much time as possible here. I'll go get that coffee."

He walks inside, pulling the heavy glass door closed behind him, and I sit in a comfortable chair and keep my eyes on the water. The sun is up, but not high in the sky yet. The water is deep blue, and churning away, as if it's a moody woman in the morning, who hasn't had her coffee yet.

I take a deep breath, pulling in the salty sea air, and feel myself relax against the cushions, already lulled by the sound of surf and the warm air swirling lightly around me.

Yes, Florida in winter is absolutely a good idea.

"Here you go," Carter says as he carries two steaming cups of coffee outside, on a tray with a variety of pastries as well.

"When did you have time to go to the grocery store?"

"I called yesterday," he says as he settles into a chair next to mine and takes a sip of coffee, crossing his ankles on the ottoman. "They stocked the kitchen and brought you some clothes as well."

I raise a brow at him over my mug. "Clothes for me?"

"A couple dresses, in case we decide to go to dinner, and some bathing suits for walking the beach. Nothing too crazy."

"You had someone shop for me."

I blink, wondering if I should be offended or touched.

"Problem?"

"I don't know," I say truthfully and reach for a cherry Danish. I bite in thoughtfully and enjoy the sweet on my tongue. "It's . . . disconcerting. The thought of having someone I don't know choose clothes for me."

"I won't do it again." It's as simple as that. I watch the breeze flutter through his dark hair. His eyes are calm. "I just wanted to surprise you. But from now on, I'll give you a heads-up so you can pack accordingly."

"I love the surprise." I pop the last bite of Danish in my mouth and sigh, sinking back farther into my chair. "And I appreciate you bringing me. I was getting very tired of winter."

"Do you enjoy the beach?"

"I don't know. I'm a midwestern girl, and we didn't get to the beach often. But I've often thought that I'd love to have a place to go in the winter, to escape the snow and the people."

"Not a city girl, either?" He does look surprised now.

"I love the city. It's exciting and fast paced. So much to see and do and learn. But sometimes, I long to be somewhere quiet, like this. I mean, isn't it nuts that after just a two-hour plane ride, we're in seventy-degree weather, pretty much alone?"

"These units are all full right now," he says with a grin. "They're privately owned, and just about everyone loves to snowbird here in the winter."

"Well, it feels like we're alone."

"You're right." He glances around thoughtfully. "I think it's because these balconies are built to be private. It's a nice place."

"Haven't you been here before?"

"I have, six months ago when Granddad passed, and I met with his attorney. I was surprised he left me so much."

"Why? You were his only grandchild."

"Because my father's still living. I assumed it would all go to him."

I shift in my chair, facing Carter. "Did he leave your dad anything?"

"Plenty of money," Carter says with a nod. "Not that he

needed more of it. The will was just a surprise, that's all. I decided to keep this unit for myself. I figured Gabby would get a kick out of coming here a few times a year."

"She would love it," I agree. "She'd also love redecorating the inside."

"It's not so bad."

I chuckle and sip my coffee. "No, but it does look like an older woman decorated it."

"Because she did," Carter says with a smile. "Grandma had a great time with it. She was able to enjoy it for two years before she passed last year."

"I'm glad. If I were you, I'd be here every weekend."

He blinks at me slowly. "That often?"

"Oh yeah. Look at this view. I mean, I know it's not practical to say *every* weekend, but I'd come as often as I could."

"Done," he says.

"What do you mean?"

"We'll come as often as we can. It may not be *every* weekend, but I bet we could manage every month."

"You're serious."

"Of course. You and Gabby can decorate it however you want."

I don't know what to say. It's like it's the easiest thing in the world, thinking so far into the future.

This could be over in a week. A month. We haven't talked about anything long term, and well, that's fine because we've only been seeing each other this way for a few weeks.

But damn it, I'm already in love with him, and now he's brought me to a condo in the very place I've longed for most of my adult life, and has offered to let me decorate it as I see fit.

I don't know what to say.

"Are you okay?" he asks with a grin.

"Fine," I reply and reach for another Danish. "I'm just fine."

HE'S GONE.

I blink in the dark, getting my bearings. I'm in the condo. The bed is cold where Carter was just a few hours ago.

It's the dead of night. I glance out the doors of the bedroom to the balcony beyond but don't see him out there.

There's a full moon tonight, lighting up the outside brightly. I pad to the closet and reach for the silky robe that was bought for me and pull it around my naked body.

There was significantly more than a few dresses and swimsuits in the closet when I came to look around this afternoon.

I won't have to pack for a trip down here anytime soon.

With the robe around me, I walk out to the living area. The space is dark, as is the kitchen, with no Carter.

But then I spot him, standing on the balcony, resting his forearms on the banister, his ankles crossed. He's wearing nothing but sweatpants, leaving his torso and feet bare.

My God, he's something to look at.

The moonlight shines on his skin, defining every muscle on his back. His arms flex as he clasps his hands together, and I feel the saliva pool in my mouth.

I've always known that Carter is handsome. But now, after getting to know him intimately, he's stunning. Sexy. Charming.

He brings out emotions in me that I've never felt before, and I was a married woman for six years.

What does that say about me?

That you didn't love Richard the way you love Carter.

A year ago, that would have been a hard pill to swallow.

Today, it's as easy as breathing.

Because it's true. I've never loved *anyone* the way I love Carter, and I'm quickly learning that I don't know him nearly as well as I thought I did. I can't wait to discover more about this complex man.

Carter calmly turns and rivets his eyes on me. I've been caught.

I grin and walk to the door, pull it open, and step outside with him, shutting the door behind me. He reaches for my hand and embraces me, kisses my palm, and presses it over his heart.

It's a gesture that's become habit for him, and it's one that makes my heart stutter, then pound in my chest.

"You left," I whisper before pressing a kiss to his bare arm. "I was worried."

"I couldn't sleep," he says softly. "Look at the way the moonlight dances on the water."

"Beautiful." I look up at his face, admiring the stubble that's grown on his sharp jawline. "I was watching the moonlight on your skin."

"Were you now?" He turns to me fully and pulls the silk sash open on my robe, exposing my nakedness before pressing me to him, skin on skin. "I have a hunger for you, Nora. It seems no matter how much I feast on you, it's never enough."

"I'm right here," I tell him and twist my fingers in his thick, dark hair. "I'm not going anywhere."

His lips lower to mine. It's a lazy kiss in the moonlight, as the surf pounds below. He's exploring my mouth, my tongue as his hands roam gently over my breasts and ribs, making me shiver in the cool night air.

"You're so damn beautiful," he says before biting my earlobe. He plants his hands on the globes of my ass and lifts me against the wall, his eyes even with mine. I feel him reach down to move the sweats out of the way, and then he's sinking inside me, and all I can do is wrap my legs around his waist, holding on for dear life.

His hips move in the same rhythm as the surf, and his eyes don't leave mine. We're quiet, even though there's certainly no one else awake or on their balconies. It seems fitting to watch each other, our gasps and heavy breathing drowned by the force of the ocean.

I can see in his eyes when he's about to lose control. I tip my forehead against his and hold on tight. "Go over."

"Come with me."

How can I ever resist him?

Chapter Eleven

~Carter~

I 've never been happier to own a property in my life. Granted, my grandfather went a bit above and beyond by buying the entire building, but being near the water fuels me in ways that the city just doesn't, which surprises me because I've never spent a significant amount of time near the beach in the past.

It seems that Nora loves it as well, which is the most important thing. Remembering the way her skin looked under the silver moonlight heats my blood. Listening to the crashing of the waves swallow her sighs of passion is a memory I'll never lose.

Yes, Nora at the beach is a wonder to behold.

If she wants to come here every weekend, I'll make it happen. Things between us have changed so quickly, and yet, I can't imagine a life without her.

I pray to the gods that I never have to know what that feels like.

I survived tragically losing love once.

I don't know that I could do it again.

I'm walking along the shore, watching what look like black pelicans fly over the waves in straight formation. The sand on the east coast of Florida is coarser than the Gulf Coast side, but no less beautiful. It's rich with shells and all kinds of things to discover after the tide.

Yes, Gabby will love it here. We'll make the trip down again soon and the women in my life can start redecorating the condo, making it into a comfortable second home for both of them. I'm excited to see what they choose.

I haven't read the letter in my pocket. Maggie gave it to me a couple of years ago, and I tucked it away, almost forgetting about it until Gabby asked to read her own letter when she had the chicken pox.

"Darcy gave this to me," Maggie said with a sad smile. *"She asked me to hold on to it and give it to you when you've fallen in love again. But only you will know when that happens, dear. So I'm passing it on to you, to keep for when the time is right."*

The time is right.

I sit on a weathered log and pull the sealed envelope out of my pocket. My name is written in Darcy's tidy handwriting.

For a while, before Maggie gave this to me, I was angry. I thought Darcy only wrote letters to Gabby, and I felt left out. I needed to hear her voice, too. I missed her, too.

And then this came to me, and I realized that it wasn't that she didn't think of me, but that we'd said all we needed to say when she was still here, and I'm grateful for that. We left nothing unsaid. I have no regrets about my time with my late wife.

I carefully open the envelope and unfold the letter.

Carter—

If you're reading this letter it's because you've had time to heal, and you've found someone special, as you should. I've been telling you for weeks now that one day you'll fall in love again, not because you've forgotten me, but because your heart has mended and is ready to be given to someone wonderful.

And I'm sure she's wonderful. She must be to win you over. You're such an incredible person, Carter. Your capacity for love, for patience, for kindness are unparalleled. You've loved me so completely, there's no more I could have asked for.

I also know that whoever she is, she loves our Gabby girl. You wouldn't accept anything less than a woman who loves our daughter as her own.

It's my deepest wish that you're happy. Truly. That you and Gabby, while always remembering me, don't dwell on the past, but live your lives to the fullest with

a beautiful person by your side. I hope you have a long,
full life together. Not that you need my approval, or my
blessing. But you have them just the same.

Love always,
Darcy

Well, if that isn't a punch to the gut, I don't know what is. I read the letter once again, then tuck it away and fiddle with the ring I have in the other pocket. I've been carrying it with me, in case an opportunity arises to get on one knee.

Yes, it's fast.

No, I don't give a fuck.

It seems my life has been on hold for five years, and I'm ready to start a new chapter with Nora. She's wonderful.

She's everything good in my life, aside from Gabby.

And I can't wait to officially make her mine.

Movement from the corner of my eye catches my attention and I turn to see Nora walking down the beach toward me, smiling as she approaches.

"Hey." She sits beside me and links her arm through mine, putting her head on my shoulder. "It's a nice morning for a walk."

"Agreed." I kiss the top of her head and breathe deep, inhaling the sweet smell of her. "You were asleep, and I didn't want to wake you."

"Well, someone kept me up half the night." She smiles up at me, her brown eyes shining. "Not that I minded."

I reach for her hand and kiss the palm, then press it to my heart.

"Are you hungry?" I ask her.

"I could eat." But we don't move. We sit where we are, watching the waves. "How many sharks do you think are in the water?"

"Plenty," I say with a laugh. "Do you want to swim in it?"

"God no." She shakes her head vehemently. "No, there's a pool for that. Is it always so warm in Florida in the winter?"

"I think this is warmer than usual. I'm not sure."

She sighs happily and leans her head against me again. "I like the way your bicep feels against my face. When do you find time to work out?"

"I fit it in," I reply. "Push-ups in my office, runs now and then."

"You do push-ups in your office?" Her gaze flies up to mine, her eyes wide. "I want to see that."

"I'm alone when I do them."

"Not anymore." She kisses my arm and then looks back out at the water. "I can't stop staring at it. It's so powerful, yet soothing at the same time. The sound alone fills me with peace."

"I understand. I love it, too. We'll come back soon with Gabby."

"When do we have to go back?" Her voice is soft, as if she dreads the idea, and I don't disagree with her. Thirty-six hours wasn't enough.

"Not until after dinner."

"Great. Let's go sit by the pool and be lazy." She stands and pulls on my hand. "I'll fix snacks."

"You're a delicious snack."

Her grin is quick and full of mischief. "You can have both."

"Deal."

THIS IS AGAINST the rules," Nora reminds me a few days later. It's early in the morning, before anyone else is in the office, and I'm kissing her at her desk. Or trying to anyway.

"Fuck the rules," I mutter and plant my lips on her neck. This spot, right here, always makes her crazy. The way her fingers tighten on my arm tells me I'm not wrong.

Rather than pull away, she chuckles. I want to take her into my office and fuck her on my desk the way I've daydreamed of more times than I'd like to count, but this isn't the time, so I pull back and clutch her hand in mine.

"Let's go out for lunch," I begin, but Nora suddenly stiffens and tugs her hand quickly out of mine. "What's wrong?"

She shakes her head once and drops into her chair.

"I'll see to that, Carter."

I glance around, and see Mary from HR walking away, down the hall to the lounge.

"Was that for her benefit?"

"Do you need anything else?" she asks rather than answer my question, and it immediately pisses me the fuck off.

"What in the hell is going on?"

"This is rule number one," she reminds me, not meeting my eyes. Her hands shake a little as she reaches for a folder. "We need to remember to stick to the rules. No hanky-panky at work."

"Screw that." My voice is hard. The rules were before I'd spent the past few weeks with her. Before I freaking fell in love with her. "Are you embarrassed about us, Nora?"

"Of course not."

"Is what we have something to be ashamed of?"

"No, that's not—"

"Because if that's the case, we'll call it right now."

"Carter, that's not what I'm saying. Of course I'm not ashamed of you. It's just not appropriate for the workplace, that's all."

"I see." I step away, hurt more deeply than I would have expected. Her rejection hit a nerve I didn't realize I had.

"Carter—"

"I don't want to speak to you just now," I say as I stride to my office. "I'll let you know if I need you."

I shut the door behind me and sit in the chair behind my desk, swiveling to look out at the city around me.

I was ready to *propose* to her. Clearly if she can't handle being affectionate at work, we're not on the same page.

How could I be so stupid? So sure that what I was feeling is reciprocated. It doesn't mean we won't ever be, but perhaps I'm rushing things.

Nora pulling away hurt. More than I want to admit.

"I QUIT."

Nora barges into my office the next day. We didn't spend the previous evening together. In fact, I've barely spoken to her since the altercation at her desk yesterday morning.

I was licking my wounds, and I needed some time to think. To adjust the plan.

Hell, my feelings were hurt and I was sulking. I can admit it.

Nora closes the door behind her and marches in, her sweet little chin in the air, and sits opposite me.

"Did you hear me?"

I arch a brow and lean on my desk. My heart is pounding. "In what capacity are you quitting? As my assistant, or my lover, companion, *everything*?"

Her lips twist and tears spring to her eyes, and I want to rush around the desk, pull her in my arms, and insist that everything's going to be fine.

But I need her answer first.

"As your assistant." She clears her throat. She's on the verge of tears. "It's the right thing to do."

"From where I'm sitting, it's *not* the right thing." What in the hell would I do without her?

"Would you rather—" She goes pale, and it destroys me.

"No." I do round the desk now and put my arms around her, lead her to the couch. "No, I don't want either to happen."

"Something has to give," she says and dabs at a tear. "And I'm seriously pissed that I'm crying. I thought I got it out of my system."

"You spent last night crying?" I'm a complete ass. Why did I think it was best to spend last night apart when we were both just miserable?

"A little," she confesses. "Carter, I can't be your girlfriend *and* your assistant. Whether we like it or not, there is a no-frat policy in this company."

"Nora, I *own* the damn company. We can do whatever the hell we want."

"So . . . what? *Do as I say, not as I do*?" She shakes her head miserably. "I hated it when my parents pulled that crap on me when I was kid, and I won't do that here. The rules apply to everyone. That's why they're there."

"They're a pain in my ass," I mutter and rub my hand over my face in frustration.

"Mary's a pain in *my* ass," she says. "That girl doesn't like me. I don't think she likes anyone, and I truly think she'll try to make things harder around here. Not that they're hard now, but you know what I mean."

"Then she's gone."

"No." She shakes her head and pats my leg. "I can't win, don't you see? Quitting my position is the right thing to do. And

I won't go far. Sienna hasn't formally hired her new assistant, so I'll take that job, and I'll assign someone new to you. But you don't get Victoria because she's twenty-six, a size four, and single. So, you get Alice, who is just as qualified, in her forties, and married with three kids."

"I didn't realize that was part of the official qualifications."

"Well, it is because I don't need to be distracted all day because I'm worried that the new assistant is trying to get in your pants."

Now that the storm is passing, I hug her and kiss the hell out of her, just because I can and I've missed her.

"Darling, no one gets in my pants but you."

"You bet your ass," she says.

"Exactly."

She laughs now and leans her forehead on mine. "Are we okay now? Because yesterday sucked monkey balls."

"That's a vivid image." I brush my fingers into her hair, soothing us both. "We were always okay. I just had a bruised ego and my feelings hurt."

"I didn't mean to hurt you." She wraps her arms around me tightly. "I promise, hurting you is the last thing I ever want to happen."

"I know."

"And I can't ever do the silent treatment again." She pulls back and glares at me now. "Ever. Don't do that. It's childish, and unfair. Call me into your office and yell at me, *anything*. Richard used to pull that shit on me, and it killed me."

"Done. I'm sorry, Nora. I won't do it again. I think I was thrown, and I didn't know how to deal with it."

"Well, any way is better than that way. So stop it."

"Yes, ma'am. Let me make it up to you."

"Do you have chocolate in here?"

I grin and walk to my desk, open the drawer, and toss her a Snickers. "It's my last one, and you're welcome to it. But that's not what I had in mind."

"Sexual favors?"

I laugh now, relieved that my pulse is settling down and all is right with my world again. "Yes, that sounds fun, too, but I was thinking I'd give us both the rest of the day off and we'd go back to the Met. Look at art. Flirt. End up in bed for those sexual favors."

"Can't." She stands, peeling the wrapper of her candy bar. "I have to go tell Sienna I'm officially working for her, and get Alice set up with HR so she can start tomorrow. This also means that I won't be able to leave on a whim anymore."

"Fucking hell."

"But," she says with a smile, "Sienna works part-time, so I shouldn't be as tied to my desk as I have been."

She's grinning at me, triumphantly. God, is it any wonder that I love her so much? Just look at her. Brown eyes shining, curvy body tucked in a smart red suit, blond hair spilling over her shoulders.

She's fucking brilliant.

And she's mine.

"Go get it all settled then," I say. "And we'll catch up later over dinner."

"I'm making spaghetti," she says as she walks to the door. "Gabby requested it."

"Sounds perfect to me."

She walks out, leaving me alone.

Chapter Twelve

~Nora~

I've gotten more done in the week since you came on with me than in the previous two years combined," Sienna says with a laugh. "Is it wrong that I'm grateful that Carter can't keep his hands off you?"

"It's not wrong. I'm happy to be working with you."

It's not a lie. Sienna is fantastic, and the past week has gone smoothly. If anything, I run out of things to see to, which has been convenient because I've had to bounce back and forth between helping Carter's new assistant and my position with Sienna.

It's not been easy to adjust. I've done the same work for so long, I didn't realize that so much of what I did was on auto-pilot. Gratefully, because Sienna is part-time, I can still help Carter out when it comes to Gabby and her many activities. In that aspect, at least, things haven't changed.

"Okay," Sienna continues, "let's have a look at—" She's interrupted by the ringing of her phone and picks it up. "Sienna. Hey, Mary."

She rolls her eyes at me, making me grin.

It's good that we're on the same page there.

"Yes, I can come to your office. Nora's with me." Sienna's eyes fly to mine. "Yes, I'll ask her to join me."

She hangs up.

"We've been called into the principal's office."

"Because we have time for this," I mutter and stand when she does. "She probably has questions about assigning Alice to Carter rather than you."

"Most likely," Sienna agrees as we walk to the elevator and go up a floor to Mary's cubicle in the HR office.

"Come with me, please," Mary says primly, leading us to a small conference room, and shuts the door behind her with a sharp click. "Have a seat."

She sets a folder at the head of the table and sits with her hands folded over it, watching us with cool blue eyes. The air of authority she's trying to present is almost laughable.

She's truly trying to make us feel like we're in trouble.

"I need to talk to both of you ladies," Mary begins. "It's come to my attention, both here at work and away from the office, that you're engaging in behavior that goes against our ethics code."

She pulls two sets of stapled papers out of her folder and gives us each one.

"If you turn to page sixteen, as I've flagged it for you, you'll see the passage I'm referring to. You both received the handbook when you first started your employment here."

Sienna and I both scan the document and then look at each other with looks of *what in the actual fuck?*

"Let me see if I have this right," Sienna says. "You're slapping us on the wrist for having relationships with Quinn and Carter?"

"That's right, as you ca—"

"Hold up," Sienna says, holding her hand up. "You have a problem with my relationship with my *husband*."

"Well, when you're in the office, you are colleagues and should behave in a professional manner."

I close the booklet and toss it on the table, then sit back in my chair and level my gaze at Mary, who's suddenly looking a little nervous.

As she damn well should be.

"You know what, Mary? I'm done with you bullying me."

"I beg your pardon," Mary demands just as Sienna snickers beside me.

"You can beg for it, but I'm not going to give it," I reply, leaning in. "First of all, Sienna is married to Quinn. They'll behave as they choose, at the office or elsewhere. And as for me? Well, I'm with Carter, and I don't care if that makes you angry, or uncomfortable. Nor do I care if you have a crush on him, and this is your way of throwing a little temper tantrum.

"We're in relationships with the owners of this firm. If you want to pursue this, I suggest you take it up with them. No, I *dare you* to take it up with them."

"What she said," Sienna says. "Nora's right, you're a bully, and a pain in my butt. If you think you can drag us in here and look down your nose at us that way, well, you have another think coming."

"The policy is clear," Mary says, her voice wavering now. "I respect that you're married to Quinn, Sienna, but there's a time and place for public displays of affection, and here in the workplace is not that time or place."

"Let's be honest," I cut in. "We're here because you're pissed at me, plain and simple. Like it or not, Carter and I *are* in a relationship, and I will not apologize for it to you or anyone else. I left my position as his assistant because of the policy. I won't stop seeing him."

"I see." Mary nods once. "Then I see no other choice but to recommend you're fired."

I laugh, not intimidated by Mary in the least. Why was I ever truly concerned about this? Behaving in a professional manner is one thing, but being worried about what Mary of all people thinks is another matter altogether.

"Okay," I say and stand. "Go ahead. Is that all?"

Without waiting for a reply, Sienna and I march out of the conference room, out of HR, and return to our floor. Once we're in Sienna's office and I've shut the door, we stare at each other and then dissolve into giggles.

It's either laugh or cry, and I've shed all the tears over this particular subject that I'm willing to.

"She has nerve," Sienna says, wiping a tear from under her eye. "What's her problem?"

"She has a crush on Carter," I reply with a deep sigh. "At least, that's the office gossip, which I hate."

"She can have a crush all day long. The man only has eyes for you," Sienna says. "You'd have to be blind not to see it."

"Yeah, well, she'll get over it. And if she doesn't, I'll recommend *she's* the one to be fired. I don't ever want to have to do that, but I won't be bullied here. I've been at this job for a decade, and I plan to be here for a decade more."

"I like you," Sienna says thoughtfully. "I mean, I already knew I liked you, but I just have to say that I respect you as well. You handled her professionally, and then when that wasn't going to work, the woman in you kicked in and stuck up for your relationship. We should all be so lucky as to have a partner like that."

"That's what you have with Quinn," I remind her.

"Oh yeah. In spades. And it makes me happy that you and Carter have the same."

TODAY GOT CRAZY.

After my dressing down by Mary, Sienna and I got slammed with a new client and didn't end up leaving the office for the day until after six. I rushed home to pack some fresh clothes and got cornered in the hallway by Christopher, whom I've barely seen in weeks.

I miss him. I promised to have dinner with him one night this week.

Then I hurried over to Carter's penthouse to get dinner going.

We didn't eat until after eight, and I felt bad for it because we were all starving. There wasn't a noodle or a piece of garlic bread left over.

Once Gabby went to bed, I wanted to fall face-first into bed myself.

But Carter had a few things to see to for work, so I tidied the kitchen while he tapped away on his laptop, and now we're finally getting ready for bed.

"Now that Gabby's asleep and your work is done, I have to tell you about what happened today," I say as I spread toothpaste on my brush and start brushing my teeth.

"Okay," he says, then whips his T-shirt over his head, one-handed, and I stop to stare. "Well?"

"Well what?" I ask with the brush still in my mouth.

"You're so classy, darling," he says with a laugh and kisses my temple. "What happened today?"

"Oh!" I hurry to finish brushing, spit in the sink, then rinse my mouth and wipe it on a towel. "So Sienna and I were called into a meeting with Mary in HR."

I wet my face and scrub it clean, then reach for my moisturizer. "And?"

"And she's a first-rate bitch, but that's neither here nor there." I'm slathering the lotion into my face, watching Carter in the mirror as he strips out of his slacks and reaches for a pair of pajama bottoms.

He never wears anything on top, God bless him.

"We were in trouble for fraternizing with you and Quinn."

That brow quirks up, the way it does when he's annoyed. "Excuse me?"

"I told you this would happen." I sigh and pump regular lotion in my hand to rub into my feet and sit cross-legged on the bed as Carter joins me, leaning his back against the headboard and watching me with concerned blue eyes. "She called us out for being affectionate at work. It was complete bullshit. I mean, I understand that she thinks it's part of her job, but I also think she was being a vindictive pain in the ass as well. She's both."

Carter nods thoughtfully, and I keep going.

"Anyway, I told her to go fuck herself."

Carter sputters, coughs, and then says, "What?"

"You heard me. I told her that Sienna and Quinn are *married*. What they do is none of her business, and that I'm in a relationship with you and if she has a problem with that, she can take it up with you."

He reaches over and takes my hand in his, then kisses my palm in that way he does and covers his heart with it.

"You take my breath away, darling."

"I'm sick of her bullying me. Of being afraid that she'll

gossip about us. So what if she does? You said it yourself that you own the damn company."

"I do," he says with a nod.

"But this is exactly why I was so intent on being careful," I explain to him, needing him to see my point of view. "I knew that it would become an issue. Carter, you're the most important part of my life. I'm absolutely crazy about you and Gabby. But I love my job, too. I *need* it. I need you both."

"I know, and I'm sorry I was so hardheaded that I didn't understand it before. And in that vein, I'm happy to report that as of today, that no-fraternization policy no longer exists."

I still and feel my eyes go wide. "Excuse me?"

"That's right. It seems while Mary was flexing her imaginary muscles with you, I was in a meeting with her boss, Quinn, and Finn. We decided to do away with that clause, given Quinn's relationship with Sienna, and mine with you. There is still a paragraph that says the workplace is to remain professional."

"As it should be," I agree and then fling myself in Carter's arms, kissing him soundly. "You did that?"

"Of course. I need you, too. Nora, I need you to come back to work for me."

"That bad, huh?"

He winces, and I feel a moment of sympathy for him.

"Alice is nice, but she's not you. I had to either redo her work or call you to fix it more than she did anything right all week. Please, I beg you, come back to me."

"Hmm, it's an interesting offer." I sit back on his knees and tap my finger to my lips, thinking it over. "I wonder if I could get a raise out of you."

"I'll pay you whatever you want."

I blink rapidly, surprised. "Maybe just a small raise. Or a bonus. You know how I love shoes, and I want to keep you happy because you love them, too."

"I'll buy you all the shoes you want."

"I rather like buying them myself."

His lips twitch. "You're independent."

"Damn skippy."

He laughs now and eases me onto the bed, on my back, and hovers over me, plucking tenderly on my lips with his teeth.

"I like an independent woman," he murmurs and kisses down my neck to where it meets my shoulder. It's my sweet spot.

Good lord, the things he does to me with those lips.

"As long as we agree on one thing."

I've lost the ability to breathe. He tugs my shirt up and over my head, then feasts on my nipples, pulling and tugging them with his lips and teeth, making me a writhing, squirming mess.

Carter pins my hands over my head with one hand and continues to torture me in the most delicious of ways with the other.

"Did you hear me?" he demands.

"I don't know."

He smiles against my skin and then looks into my eyes. He looks happy. Not a little possessive.

"We need to agree on one thing."

"I'll agree to just about anything."

He smiles again and plants a sweet kiss on the tip of my nose.

"You don't know what it is yet."

"Just consider it a yes."

He shakes his head slowly, and, letting go of my hands, slowly kisses down my body, uncovering and shedding clothes as he goes. My waist is good and thoroughly examined. My outie belly button is adored.

He skims his lips down my thighs and lifts my leg to press wet kisses behind my knee.

Holy Jesus on a cracker, I had no idea my knee was such a hot spot.

"Whoa," I breathe, and he smiles at me triumphantly.

"Like that?"

"It sends electricity right through me."

"That's the goal." He makes his way down my calf to my foot and settles in to give me a thorough massage.

"Hey, don't get hung up there. You were on a roll."

"We have all night," he murmurs and kisses my big toe.

Thank God I just got out of the shower.

I want him to keep going on his sensual exploration, but damn, that feels good.

I'm in desperate need of a pedicure.

Finally, he switches to the other foot, pays it the same attention, and then works his way back up again.

"This knee isn't as sensitive as the other one," he says after kissing the soft skin. "Interesting."

"I want to touch you, too."

"You will."

Sometimes, Carter takes his sweet time when it comes to sex. Not that I'm complaining. He's just not one for a quickie.

At least, not that I'm aware of.

"What are you thinking about that has you frowning?" he asks before planting a kiss on my hip.

"We've never really done the quickie thing."

He blinks in surprise. "Would you prefer that?"

"No, not necessarily. It just occurred to me, that's all."

"Next time," he promises and kisses my rounded belly. I don't have a flat stomach like Sienna. I'm not a stick figure. It's something I've grown to accept about myself.

Carter doesn't seem to mind in the least.

"Oh my," I murmur as he kisses down my pubis and spreads my legs wide before nudging his shoulders between them and settles in, in that way he does, to pay respects to this part of me.

"You like this." It's said with the confidence of a lover who's been there before and knows what he's doing.

It's sexy as hell.

I have to grip onto the pillow when he slips his tongue through my folds and up to my clit, where he lazily circles and waits for me to lose my damn mind.

It doesn't take long.

Then, rather than leaving it at that, he sinks a finger inside me, wraps those lips around me, and tugs gently.

And I rear up off the bed, doing my best to not call out his name, in fear of waking Gabby.

She's a ways away, but I don't want to risk it.

"I fucking love the way your body responds to me." His voice is rough now, heavy with lust and yearning. "It's a damn miracle every time. I'll never get enough of it."

"Can't help it," I pant and reach for him, needing him over me. In me. "Your fault. Now come up here."

"I won't turn that down." He grins, showing off the dimple, and rests between my legs, brushing my hair off my cheeks as he nudges me with the head of his cock. "Do you have any idea what you do to me?"

"Pretty good idea." I kiss him lightly, glorying in the weight of him. "I want you, Carter."

"More," he demands, his hands fisting in my hair, and I know exactly what he wants.

"I *need* you," I reply. He slips inside me, hard and smooth, and stills, watching me with his hot blue eyes. "Only you."

"Damn right." He kisses my palm and plants it over his heart as he moves, picking up the pace as if he can't control himself. He's a man possessed, chasing after his own release. My hips are moving, rising and falling with him. He pulls my legs up around his hips, higher, so he can push even farther inside me and I go blind as my release washes over me.

I bite his shoulder to keep from crying out, and Carter buries his face in my neck, groaning as his own release washes over him.

Once we've found our breath, and I can see again, he rolls to his side, tucking me in against him and kissing my hair.

"Oh yeah, you never said what I have to agree to," I remind him. I feel him smile.

"Mine," he says simply. "You have to agree to be mine."

"I already am."

Chapter Thirteen

~Nora~

Are you mad at me?"

I stare at Christopher across the table at our favorite restaurant in Manhattan. We've just ordered our greasy burgers and fries, and he's sipping on a Coke, watching me with worried hazel eyes, his brows lowered.

"I mean, sort of," he admits. "No, you know what? We've been friends for a long time, and I've been with you through a lot of shit, so I'm just going to be brutally honest here."

"Okay."

"Yeah, I'm mad. I've never pegged you as the kind of friend who would drop the people closest to you just because you have a boyfriend."

I stare at him, dumbfounded.

"What in the hell are you talking about? I'm here with you right now."

"I've barely heard from you in a month," he points out. "And that was only because I happened to pin you down in the hallway of your apartment. You never text me unless I text first. I just never expected this from you, and it hurts my feelings."

Seems all I do is hurt people's feelings these days.

"Okay, that's fair. You're right, and I'm sorry. I'm never home, and I haven't reached out to you, and I'm truly sorry for all that. I didn't mean to do that, and I'm *not* the type of person to abandon my friends for a man."

"Could have fooled me," he says, sulking into his Coke.

"Well, now you've pointed it out to me and I can fix it. And I promise, I *will* fix it, Christopher. You're my best friend, and I adore you. That's how this works, right?"

"Yes, that's true. I'm not trying to be a dick here, I was just worried about you, *and* happy for you. You look really good for the first time maybe since I've known you."

"I'm doing really well," I say with a nod and sit back as the waitress delivers our food. I reach for the ketchup and squirt a trough of it next to my fries, then a spiral on my burger and pass it to Christopher, who does the same.

"How are you getting along with Gabby?"

"So far, so good."

"Like I said, I think it's great. Just don't forget about me. I love you, too, you know."

"I know." I reach over to take his hand in mine. "I know, and I love you, too. I'll make a better effort, I promise."

"Thank you."

"Now, what's new with you? Are you seeing anyone?"

"I was seeing another dancer named Damon, but he turned out to be a schmuck."

"I've never liked the name Damon." I chew on a fry, thinking it over. "Isn't that weird? It's not like I know anyone I dislike with the name."

"It sounds like demon to me," Christopher says with a smile. "But I'll never admit that to anyone besides you."

"So he's not the guy for you."

"No. He was just after my body. Which, I mean, how can you blame him?"

"How indeed."

"Right? I met another guy at the supermarket the other day, so we'll see if he calls me."

"Wait. You gave your number to a guy at the market?"

"How else am I supposed to meet people?" he demands and takes a bite of his burger. "This is worth every single calorie."

"I don't know if the market is any better than a club." I chew thoughtfully. I need more ketchup. "I mean, it's a perfect stranger."

"Honey, they're all perfect strangers until you get to know them. I doubt he's a serial killer. He's too hot for that."

"Ted Bundy was hot," I remind him. "And charming."

"But he didn't kill men."

"So?" I laugh now and wipe my mouth with my napkin. "What does that have to do with anything?"

"I dunno, I'm just saying. Ted Bundy was heterosexual."

"I'm certain there have been gay serial killers. I could google it."

I reach for my phone, but Christopher shakes his head. "No, I don't want to know."

"This is New York. Serial killer is your best-case scenario if he's crazy."

"Jesus, Nora, you make me never want to date again. And that's just sad. A man has needs."

"Ew." I wrinkle my nose and toss a fry at him, which he catches and pops in his mouth. "I don't want to know about your needs."

"I want to know about yours," he says, leaning in closer. "Give me all the details on Carter. That man is hotter than July in Hades."

"He's pretty hot."

"And he has long fingers, and that's a good sign."

"Don't ruin this for me," I say with a laugh and sip my chocolate shake. "Seriously, Christopher, don't be gross about it."

"Who's being gross? I just want to know the scoop, that's all."

This is very different from talking with Sienna and London. Is it because I know Christopher so well that I want to clam up and keep it all for myself?

"Give me *something*."

"He's just . . . really good at it," I say at last. "Like, really good."

"Hmm, lots of practice then," he says with a knowing nod and I scowl at him.

"Darcy died five years ago, and he says there's been no one since then."

"Right." Christopher busts up laughing, slapping the table, as if I just told him the funniest joke ever. "Trust me, a man doesn't go five years without some nookie."

"You don't know that." I hear the defensiveness in my voice, and I don't care. "He works a lot, and he has a young daughter. Maybe he was too busy."

"Or he's lying."

"Jesus, Chris, don't start that shit with me. I don't have a reason to think Carter's lied to me. That's not cool."

"Okay, I'm sorry. You're right, I don't know him from Adam. Maybe he *was* a monk for five years. It's unlikely, but possible."

"Just because you can't keep it in your pants—"

"Okay, okay." He holds his hands up in surrender. "I'm sorry. Honest."

"Okay." I sigh and drop the last of my burger in the basket. "He's not like Richard. He's not a jerk."

"Good. He'd better not be, or I'll kick his ass. I may be gay, but I've got guns, and I know how to use them."

"I didn't know you owned firearms."

He rolls his eyes and then flexes his biceps. "These guns, Nora."

"Oh, right."

I DIDN'T SLEEP well last night. It seems I've become used to sleeping with Carter, and without him to snuggle up to, I can't turn my brain off.

It's a problem.

I mean, it's not like I have to spend every single night with the man. We're allowed to have nights apart.

I'll adjust.

I've just started my computer when Carter walks into the office, looking fresh from a shower but tired around the eyes.

Maybe he didn't sleep well either?

"Good morning," he says as he walks around my desk, pulls me out of my chair, and covers my mouth with his own, kissing me silly.

"Well, good morning to you, too," I say when he finally lets me up for air.

"I missed you last night."

I grin and brush my fingers through his hair. He needs a haircut. "I missed you, too. But I had a nice time with Christopher. It was good to catch up."

"I'm glad." He kisses the tip of my nose. "Gabby was giving me some grief this morning."

"Why?"

"Because she's almost a teenager?" He shrugs a shoulder. "Who knows."

"Moods. We all have them."

"She has more than her own share." He pulls away and turns toward his office. "Dinner tonight?"

"It's a date."

He winks, and I sit back down, just as my cell phone rings.

"Geez, it's a busy morning," I mutter and read the caller ID. Great. It's my mom.

If I don't answer, she'll just call back. Might as well get it over with.

"Good morning, Mom."

"Hello, Nora," she says stiffly. It's always been this way with her. She's held me at arm's length for as long as I can remember. "How are you today?"

"I'm doing well. How are you, Mom?"

"Well, I'm fine. My back's been killing me, and I've had the vertigo again."

I cradle the phone, resigned to listening to her list of ailments. "I'm sorry to hear that."

"It's not as bad as it was when I was going through the chemo. Not that you would know because you didn't come home when I was suffering."

I close my eyes and bite my lip. I was newly employed here, trying to establish my career and make my way in the city with Richard. It wasn't that I wasn't worried about her. I called every day.

But all she remembers is that I wasn't there.

"How's Dad?" I try to sound cheerful.

"He's just fine. I think I've talked him into having that hip replacement. Now that Richard's moved back to town, and I have some help, it won't be that big of an imposition."

And there it is.

I square my shoulders, mentally preparing for the verbal beating I'm about to take.

"Well, then it sounds like it's good timing" is all I say.

"You know, you really should come home and make amends with your husband."

"Ex-husband," I remind her, my voice colder now. "Richard is my ex-husband."

"A technicality," she says, brushing me aside. "You made vows to the man, Nora Jean, and your father and I expect you to stand by those vows."

It's always the same lecture. Every fucking time.

"Now," she continues, "I know he made some mistakes."

"He screwed another woman for a *year and a half*," I remind her coldly. "I'd say that's more than a mistake."

"And why did he do that, you tell me," she counters. "Because you all but abandoned him, Nora. What's a man to do when his wife's too busy working for someone else? So busy that she's barely home. I raised you better than that. I taught you how to make a home and care for a husband."

"You taught me to be small," I reply softly. "And I won't ever do that, Mom. You're happy with your life in Ohio, and I respect that. I really do. But I don't want that for me. I will never be content as a housewife, and it's not *my* fault that Richard's penis found its way into another woman for eighteen months straight before I found out about it."

"Watch your mouth. Maybe if you'd been paying attention to Richard rather than giving all your time to that law firm, you would have seen it sooner."

"Seeing it sooner makes it okay, Mom? Is that what you're saying?"

"I'm saying that divorce isn't the answer. It's not like he ever laid his hands on you."

"I can't do this with you," I say at last, ending the conversation. "I love you, and I hope you're doing well. I honestly do. Now, I have to get to work. Good-bye, Mom."

I hang up and lay my head on my desk, my face cradled in the crook of my arm.

How did I come from a woman like that? How can our views be so drastically different?

And how could *any* parent think it's okay for her daughter to stick with a man who unapologetically cheated on her?

I don't know. Because if it were Gabby, I'd want to kill any asshole who would *dare* treat her so recklessly.

So if my parents want to choose Richard over me, I say let them. It's not like I've ever had a close relationship with them, and if they take his side over mine, well, it's their loss.

Not mine.

"I KNOW YOU want to go out for dinner," I say as Carter and I walk out of the office to his car. "But I had a hell of a day. Can we just go home?"

"Which home?" he asks as he opens the door for me.

"Either is fine. Yours, if you like."

He lowers into the car with me and nods. "Absolutely. How about pizza for dinner?"

"That's perfect. Thank you."

"Spending the evening in with you is never a hardship, darling." He kisses my knuckles and pulls out into traffic.

I've been fighting a headache all day. It's so bad that my teeth ache, which is never fun. I didn't eat well today, instead trying to stay busy so I wouldn't get upset about my conversation with my mother, but it stuck with me all day.

I hate that I let her get to me that way.

"Wanna talk about it?" Carter asks as he turns into his parking garage.

"Yeah, when we get settled upstairs."

He nods patiently and escorts me up. We already have a routine whenever we get home. We drop off our bags, slip out of our coats, and stow them away. I kick out of my heels and pad to the bedroom where I change out of my suit into yoga pants and a sweatshirt.

I throw my hair up into a ponytail with a headband and go to the kitchen, where Carter's filling two glasses with wine.

"I ordered the pizza," he says as he passes me a glass. "Pepperoni and extra cheese."

"My favorite." I smile at him as I sit on the couch and let out a long, relieved sigh. "This is exactly what I needed. Where's Gabs?"

"With Maggie this evening," he says. "She called and asked if she could stay over there tonight because I'm mean."

I snort. "Right. So mean. It's a school night."

"I know. Quinn's going to pick her up and take her to school in the morning."

"Hmm."

"You don't agree with that decision?" He cocks his head, watching me.

"I didn't say that. It's really none of my business."

"Yes, it is." His voice is soft.

"I guess I feel like giving her what she wants when she's acting out isn't going to change the behavior. It'll only reinforce that if she's a brat, she'll get whatever she wants."

"You're right. I know you're right. But she was on my last nerve this morning, and to be perfectly honest, the thought of having an evening without her sounded fantastic. Which makes me the worst father in the history of the world."

"Hardly." I reach over and pat his shoulder. "Pretty sure it makes you human. Kids are tough, and you're a single dad. Taking an evening off isn't the end of the world. But making things tough for her isn't the end of the world for her, either."

"Sometimes punishing her feels more like a punishment for *me*," he confesses.

"Totally," I agree. I've spent plenty of time with Gabby when she's been punished. It's not fun. "It'll all work out. Unfortunately, the next few years, or ten, are the hardest."

"Awesome." He pulls my feet in his lap and starts rubbing. The sound that comes from me is a cross between a moan and a purr. "So tell me what happened today."

"My mom called shortly after you arrived this morning." I lean my head back on the pillows and let myself relax into the foot rub. "Like you, it always puts me in a mood after I speak with my parents."

"What did she say?"

"It's her check-in call," I explain. "It happens a few times a year whether we need it or not. I had a feeling it would be coming soon. She basically tells me all about her many medical ailments."

"I didn't know your mom was sick."

"She's not. She just thinks she is." I shrug a shoulder. "I mean, yes, she did have stage one breast cancer about ten years ago, but she's fine now. She's always been a bit of a hypochondriac. She's gone through three doctors in ten years because they refuse to continue seeing her."

"Gotcha."

"Anyway, she also likes to browbeat me into going back to Richard."

Carter's hands still on my feet, and I crack one eye open to look at him.

"Why would they want you to do that?"

"I told you. Divorce is wrong. She still refers to him as my husband."

His eyes shrink to slits. "Does she."

"Don't worry, I correct her. It's the same argument every time. She insists I should come home and grovel for my ex-husband to take me back, and I tell her there's no chance in hell that lying son of a bitch is ever going to be part of my life again. Then I get pissed and cut the call short."

"Sounds lovely, darling."

"It's a blast."

I sigh as he switches to the other foot. "I could get used to this. It's not a bad way to end the day."

"Move in with me."

My eyes fly open, meeting his.

"Excuse me?"

"I've been meaning to talk to you about this. It makes sense for you to move in here. You have to go to your place every few days for clean clothes, or to do your laundry. It just makes sense to have one place."

I frown. "You want me to move in because it's convenient?"

"Yes." I pull my feet out of his lap. "No. Not just because of that. Of course I'd like to have you here every day. I hate sleeping without you."

"No."

He cocks a brow. "No?"

"No, thank you," I repeat. "I truly appreciate the offer, but I like having my place. It's not that big of a deal to get clothes and stuff."

Okay, it is a pain in the ass, but I'll be damned if I'll move in here because it's convenient. I got married for the same reason, and look where that got me.

"I'm not trying to hurt your feelings," I say and climb into his lap, straddling him. "Honest. I'm just not ready for that kind of a big change yet. I like things the way they are for now."

"Okay." He grips my hips and smiles up at me just as the doorbell rings. "We're assuming this position again after dinner."

"I look forward to it."

Chapter Fourteen

~Carter~

I said no."

I can feel it coming on. The headache from hell is settling in nicely right behind my left eye socket. She's also sitting in the back seat of my car while I drive the three of us to Maggie's house for Sunday family dinner.

"I don't understand why you're so mean," Gabby says. The girl's been jumping on my last nerve for days. She's pouty, surly, stubborn, and impossible.

If this is what the rest of her teen years are going to look like, I'm shipping her off to boarding school.

Okay, so I'd miss her within ten minutes, but this is ridiculous.

"I'm mean because I'm your parent, and it's my job to protect you, not be your best friend," I explain for the fifth time today. "You don't need an Instagram account, and that's the end of it."

"*All* my friends have one," she argues. "Like, every single one of them. I'm the *only* one who doesn't."

"Well, then I guess you're the only one in the whole universe with a father who doesn't think it's appropriate for a twelve-year-old to have an Instagram account. You've already stretched your phone privileges. Do you want to go back to the old way of doing things, where you don't have your phone at all unless you're away from home without me?"

Gabby sighs heavily. "No."

"I didn't think so."

I pull into Maggie's driveway, and Gabby launches herself out of the car, slamming the door and hurrying inside before I can even cut the engine.

"You're leaving town tomorrow," Nora reminds us both. She turns to me and purses her lips. "It's gonna be fun. Yay, me."

"I can have Maggie or one of the brothers keep her," I offer, but Nora's already shaking her head.

"No, it's fine. I've kept her plenty of times. I just don't understand the sudden regression to the attitude she had last year. Maybe it's me. Maybe she's having an issue with us being together."

"It could be a number of things," I reply and reach over to squeeze her hand in encouragement. "I'll see if I can get her back in with her therapist this week. Maybe she'll talk to a professional because she sure won't talk to me."

"I hope so," Nora says as we step out of the car and walk inside. Quinn and Finn are both in the kitchen with their mother, helping her put the finishing touches on dinner. Sienna and London are sitting at the island, sipping wine, and Gabby is sulking in the living room, her nose in her phone, watching YouTube.

"What's wrong with her?" Finn asks, gesturing to my daughter.

"Your guess is as good as mine," I reply and open the fridge, praying Maggie stocked up on some beer for today.

Of course she did.

"Just one," I say to Nora with a wink. "I could use it."

"I can always drive home." She kisses my shoulder as she walks over to greet Maggie with a hug. "How can I help?"

"The boys help cook," Maggie says with a smile. "So you just pour a glass of wine and relax with my girls."

"If you're sure," Nora says with surprise and joins Sienna and London with a glass of wine. I watch as Gabby glares at Nora's back and decide here and now that I need to have a heart-to-heart with my little girl.

Before I throttle her.

"Here," Maggie says, passing me a potato masher. "You're in charge of the potatoes. You always get the milk-to-butter ratio just right."

"Hear that," I say to Finn as I step to the counter next to him. "She likes my potatoes best."

"That's because you're a potato head," Finn says cheerfully, cutting vegetables for a salad.

Gabby pushes to her feet from the couch and wanders over to the wall of photos Maggie's had on display for years. Family photos, of her children as they grew up, and newer wedding photos from Finn's and Quinn's weddings.

But Gabby stops at Darcy's high school graduation photo and says, "My mom was superpretty. I don't think my dad could ever find anyone prettier than my mom was."

My eyes lock with Nora's. She's not hurt. If anything, her brown eyes are filled with humor, touched with concern.

Gabby's determined to swipe at Nora, and I'm going to get to the bottom of it.

"Maggie, I think these potatoes are ready. I'm going to have a conversation with my daughter."

"Thank you, dear" is all Maggie says as I round the kitchen counter, take Gabby's arm in my hand, and pull her to the guest bedroom farthest from the kitchen.

"What in the hell is wrong with you?" I demand after closing the door.

"I'm just saying Mom was pretty. Am I not allowed to say that?"

"Of course you can say that, but your tone is hurtful and you're aiming shots at Nora, trying to make her feel uncomfortable, and that's *not* okay."

"Because she's your favorite?"

I sigh and drag my hand down my face in agitation. "No, because she's a guest here and will be made to feel welcome. That includes you being kind, Gabby. Seriously, what's going on with you?"

"Nothing." She clams right up, crossing her arms over her chest, and I'm simply at the end of my rope with her.

"Either you act with kindness, or you can stay back here all evening."

"Fine." She plants her ass on the bed stubbornly. "I'm not hungry, anyway."

She's going to be the death of me.

"If you stay in here, you do so without your phone."

She rolls her eyes and stomps out of the room, back to the couch, and shoves her nose back in the screen.

"So what's up, buttercup?" Quinn asks Gabby from the kitchen.

"Yeah, do we need to take another trip to Martha's Vineyard?" Finn asks. "I'm sure there are some winter activities I can put you in."

"No," Gabby says, shaking her head, and I give her the look that says *I'm at the end of my rope with you, and if you don't want to be grounded for a month, you'll fix the attitude.* "No thanks."

Conversation swirls around me as we finish getting dinner ready and on the table. The girls are laughing and planning a shopping day for next week. I love that Nora fits right in, as if she's the last puzzle piece of this family. As easy as can be.

"Dinner's ready," Maggie announces happily. "We really need to do more family dinners. It's such a joy to have all my kids with me at once."

"Yeah, with *just* our family," Gabby mutters.

"So are you on your period?" Quinn asks, then gets slapped by his wife on the arm.

"You don't ask a girl that," she says.

"What?" Quinn asks, rubbing his arm. "She's acting like she is, and it's annoying. I love you, squirt, but you need to tone down the angry preteen thing a bit. It's out of control."

"No one gets it," Gabby says with a dramatic sigh. "You all just hate me."

And with that, she tosses her phone on the table and runs to the guest room, slamming the door behind her.

"So this week's gonna be fun," Nora says before popping a green bean in her mouth. "Carter's leaving for a few days. Lucky me."

"I'll cancel the trip," I offer, but Nora's already shaking her head.

"I've dealt with this from her before. We'll be okay."

"Girls her age are going through a lot," Maggie says. "Hormones and changes. And despite loving Nora, I'm sure she's confused about how she feels about her dad having a life. Kids think our worlds revolve around them, and when something different comes into the picture, it's tough for them."

"Are you a shrink?" Finn asks his mom. "Because you're pretty smart."

"I raised three children," she reminds him with a wink. "And I spend a lot of time with our Gabby. She's going to be okay."

I need to have a real conversation with my daughter, and not one out of anger. It needs to happen when we're both calm, so I can figure out what's bothering her so badly. It's clear she's suddenly having a problem with Nora's place in my life, but just a couple of weeks ago, she was cool as can be about it.

What's changed?

And what am I going to do about it?

I SHOULDN'T HAVE come on this fucking trip. It's been a cluster from the minute I left the house this morning.

I kissed Nora good-bye, then walked across the penthouse to Gabby's room, expecting to kiss her good-bye as well. I thought she'd still be asleep, but when I opened her door, she was awake and dressed, packing a suitcase.

"Good morning."

"Morning, Daddy." She smiled sweetly and continued to pack that bag.

"I have questions," I said, leaning my shoulder on the doorjamb. "Why are you up so early and why are you packing a suitcase?"

"Well, I thought I'd just go stay with Grandma while you're gone," she said, as if she's twenty-two rather than twelve. "You know, give Nora a break and all."

"That's not possible, Gabs," I replied, reminding myself to stay calm. "Grandma's going out of town for a few days with her friends. If you'd stayed at the table for dinner last night, you would have known that."

She frowned and tossed a pair of socks on the bed. "Oh."

"Nora's totally fine spending a couple of days with you. It'll be fun to have some girl time."

"I guess."

"Hey, we need to talk, Gabs." I checked the time on my watch and winced. "I have to go to catch this flight, but when I get home we're going to have a calm conversation about what's bothering you. We need to fix this."

"You should go," she murmured softly. I kissed her head and tugged her in for a hard hug before hurrying out. The rest of the day wasn't much better.

Late flights and close calls on the connection in Denver. Finally, I landed in Sacramento around noon local time and was stuck in meetings the rest of the day.

I'm exhausted. I just want to go back to the hotel, order room service, and crash. The room service will happen, but I have a couple hours of work left still.

I usually enjoy the business trips, but I miss Nora, and I'm worried about Gabby. I belong in New York.

I've just pushed through the hotel door and tossed my briefcase on the bed when my cell rings.

It's Gabby.

"Hey, Gabs."

"I don't understand why you're trying to ruin my life."

I frown and tug my tie loose.

"I think it's in my job description. What's going on?"

"When are you coming home?" she demands.

"Wednesday."

"Oh my God, I hate my life!"

And with that, she hangs up on me and I lower to the side of the bed, hang my head in my hands for five seconds, and then call Nora.

"Hey." One word, but her voice is full of stress. I want to reach through the phone and pull her to me.

"What's going on?" My voice is soft. I need to stay calm so I can calm them down. At least, that's the plan.

"Well, quite a lot, actually. I had to pick Gabby up from school early because she swore at a teacher and has been suspended through tomorrow."

I narrow my eyes. "What did she say?"

"I believe it went something like *you're not the boss of me, so you can fuck right off.* More or less."

"Jesus," I mutter.

"So I brought her home, and she immediately started playing with her phone."

"But she doesn't get her phone," I remind her.

"I took it away, and she lunged for me, Carter."

I still, sure I've heard her wrong. "Excuse me?"

"Yeah, she tried to hit me." Her voice is shaky, and the pit in my stomach just grew four sizes. "She's *never* done that before. And for the first time since I've known her, I'm scared of her. She's suddenly so aggressive and just *awful.* I mean, I know I'm stronger, and that you'd always back me if something were to happen, but I'm *so* disappointed. Not to mention, I'm worried about her. Why is this all coming out now? Why is she so damn angry?"

Her voice cracks, killing me.

"Okay, honey. It's okay. Where is she now?"

"In her room."

"And her phone?"

"In my hand."

"Good. If she tries *anything* else, and I'm talking so much as looks at you sideways, you call Finn. He'll come get her. I'm leaving first thing in the morning. I'd go right now, but it's a six-hour trip, and by the time I got there you'd both be asleep anyway."

"I hate that you have to cut your trip short."

"I don't. I need to be there, to take care of both of you. I'll be home by noon. And I'm serious when I say call Finn if you need him. He won't hesitate to come over, and he doesn't live far."

"I know." It's a whisper. God, I want to be there more than I want to breathe.

"I'm so sorry."

"It's not your fault, but, Carter, we need to figure this out. She's miserable, and it's not just a random mood. I can't get her to talk to me. I don't know what's happened."

"We'll figure it out," I assure us both. "Thank you, for everything. I'll see you tomorrow."

"Okay." She pauses, and I think she's going to say something else, but she doesn't. "Good night."

"Good night, darling."

She ends the call, and I immediately call Finn, filling him in on this evening's events.

"Jesus, Carter. What the hell is up her ass?"

"I don't know, but we're going to find out. I'll be home tomorrow, but in the meantime, I told Nora to call you if Gabby tries anything else."

"I can go get her now regardless," he offers.

"It sounds like she's holed up in her room. I suspect that's where she'll stay until I get there. But if you'd check in with Nora, I'd appreciate it."

"You got it," he says without hesitation, and I'm grateful for him and the entire Cavanaugh family all over again. "Anything you need, you know that."

"I know, and I'm grateful. See you soon."

I hang up, open my computer, and send off emails to our clients here in Sacramento, letting them know I've had a family emergency at home and will be leaving for New York first thing in the morning. Then I call Maggie, wincing when I see what time it is on the East Coast.

"Hello, dear," she says. She sounds wide awake. I just need to vent, to get Maggie's insight. She spends as much time with Gabby as I do, maybe more. I hope she can shed some light on this abrupt change of mood in Gabby.

"Hey. I need to talk. About Gabby."

"I'm all ears."

Chapter Fifteen

~Nora~

I hate you!" Gabby screams before slamming her bedroom door in my face. I tip my forehead against the smooth wood and sigh heavily.

There is not enough wine in the world for this.

"Gabby, you have to give me your phone."

The door is yanked open and Gabby throws her phone down the hallway, glares at me, and slams the door again.

Awesome.

Thankfully, the phone didn't break. I pick it up on my way to the kitchen, where I pour the biggest glass of wine I've ever seen, and go into the living room. I set Gabby's phone on the coffee table next to my own and sit back with another heavy sigh.

I've had some challenging days in my thirty-four years of life. I've been yelled at. I've been the one yelling.

But I don't think anything in the world compares to the venom a twelve-year-old can spew in your face.

Maybe I should call my own mother and apologize for once being twelve myself.

That would shock the hell out of her.

I smirk and take another sip of wine then notice Gabby's phone light up with a notification.

I reach for it and feel my eyebrows hit my hairline. It's a notification from Instagram.

Insta-fucking-gram.

The same Instagram that her father forbade her from downloading onto her phone.

"Oh, Gabs. What are you doing?"

I try to open the app, but her phone is locked. Tapping in the first four digits of her birthday opens it easily enough, and I start to comb through her phone.

Starting with the 'gram.

"Jesus."

The photos she's posted are harmless enough. Selfies of herself in the car, at Maggie's, at home. Photos of food, and shoes. It seems she really loves food.

There are even photos from London's show.

Nothing bad, thank God.

But when I open her DMs, I'm absolutely freaking horrified.

There are some messages from kids she knows at school, mostly just asking her what she's doing, if she knew that so-

and-so was dating so-and-so. But then there are the messages from *grown-ass men.*

I set my wine aside and lean forward, gobbling up every word.

There have to be ten or more of them.

Different men, contacting Gabby, whose account is *not* set to private, to tell her she's cute. To ask for more photos.

And she fucking *sent them.*

No nudes that I can see, thank Jesus. But more selfies. Lips puckered. Sly smiles.

She's twelve, not twenty-three, for fuck's sake.

One guy by the name of JaCoBsLaDdEr2001 seems to be her favorite. She's chatted with him for days. Going back before she even asked if she could have the social media app.

It seems she downloaded it long ago, then asked if it was okay.

I guess Gabby goes by the motto of *ask for forgiveness, not permission.*

Some of the content has expired, so I can't see exactly what she's said, but then I see that he gave her a phone number.

So I close out of the app and look at her texts.

Yep, there he is.

New York number.

"Fucking hell," I mutter. He's sent *tons* of photos, including dick pics, and asked her for the same.

But she refused.

She did, however, tell him that her dad is out of town and offered him this address so he could come over.

I'll sneak you in, she says.

"Like hell you will."

I want to call this asshole and tell him to stay the fuck away from Gabby. I'll kill him before I'll let him touch her.

But before I can, the doorbell rings.

"You're an idiot to ring the bell." I stomp to the door and jerk it open. "You can't exactly sneak in, you little son of a bitch, when you ring the bell."

But it's not a pedophile standing in the doorway.

It's Finn.

"Not sneaking," he says with a frown.

"Sorry." I step back and let him in, then return to the couch. "What's up?"

"Carter asked me to check in with you. Rather than call, I thought I'd stop by. Are you okay?"

"Just peachy."

He stands and watches me for a moment. "I'm going to check on our girl."

"Help yourself. Good luck that she doesn't throw something at your head or try to slap you across the face."

"For fuck's sake," he mutters as he walks away. He's only gone a few moments when he returns. "She's out cold."

"I'm sure the tantrums she's thrown all day exhausted her."

"Wanna talk about it?"

I shrug one shoulder, then pass Gabby's phone to Finn. "First, have a look at this."

He starts to read, then his brows plummet in a scowl as he pages through.

"Open Instagram, too."

"I didn't think she was allowed—"

"She's not," I interrupt and offer him an ironic grin. "Seems she does what she wants."

Once he's had enough of the phone, he sets it aside and rubs his hands over his face. "Do you have any more of that wine?"

"Sure." I move to go get him some, but he shakes his head and gestures for me to stay where I am, then stands to get it himself.

"What else happened today?"

"So much. I didn't find out about the phone stuff until just before you arrived. And trust me when I say, I don't feel guilty for invading her privacy by going through her phone."

"Nor should you," he says, his voice calm again, as he sits across from me with his wine. "She's twelve, Nora. And you're here taking care of her. You didn't invade anything."

"I got a call from the school today." I walk him through the day's events, telling basically the same story I told Carter earlier this evening.

When I've finished, he sets his wine aside and leans his elbows on his knees.

"I can't believe she was going to strike you."

"She was so mad," I murmur, shaking my head in disbelief myself. "I've never seen her like that."

"Well, you did everything right."

"I don't know if I'm cut out for this," I admit and stand to walk to the wall of windows and stare out at the city. "I mean, I know that Carter's a package deal. I've been around for a long time. I guess I just didn't realize how different it would be to fill a parent role, versus helping and picking up the slack when Carter needed me as his assistant."

I turn to look at Finn. He's so calm, so collected.

"Obviously I'm doing something very wrong because Gabby's done nothing but show me that she can't stand me being in her life for the past week. I don't know what happened. It's like a switch flipped, and she's just angry all the time. That little show she put on at Maggie's during dinner yesterday is just the tip of the iceberg."

"It's a phase," he says.

"What if I'm not cut out to be a mom?"

There. I said it. The one sentence I haven't been able to admit out loud.

"I think all parents, biological or otherwise, ask themselves that very question every day," Finn says with a kind smile. "Parenthood is tough. And Gabby's a joy in my life, but she's not easy."

"No." I sit again and feel tears threaten.

"Have you voiced your concerns to Carter?"

"No way." I shake my head and pull a pillow into my lap, gripping it tightly in my fist. "I don't want him to think that

I'm second-guessing what we have. It's just, I worry that I'm not good at this. That I'm not what Gabby and Carter need."

"I think it's been a really rough spell, and that things will get better. You need to be honest with Carter. And Gabby, for that matter. The way she's behaving is absolutely *not* okay, and it's extreme, even for her. Carter will take care of it tomorrow. In the meantime, get some sleep."

"After that text from Jacob's Ladder, I'll be sleeping on the couch with a knife so I can cut his dick off if he tries to get anywhere near that little girl."

"There, now. I think you're great parent material. He won't get in here. Gabby didn't give him the code to the elevator, and unless he's Spider-Man and can scale skyscrapers, he can't get up here."

"Thank God. What is she thinking?"

"She's not," he says simply. "That's the problem. She's intent on acting out. We'll get to the bottom of it."

"I hope so. Thanks for stopping by. I feel better."

"It's my pleasure. I'm ten minutes away, even with traffic, so you just call if you need anything else before Carter gets here tomorrow."

I nod and walk him to the door. Finn surprises me by pulling me in for a strong hug.

"You got this, Nora."

"Thanks."

I HAVEN'T SEEN hide nor hair from Gabby all morning.

Which, if I'm being honest, hasn't hurt my feelings in the least.

Despite Finn's encouraging words last night, I slept on the couch. Not just in case anyone tried to get in, but in case Gabby tried to get *out*.

At this point, I wouldn't put it past her.

I heard her go to the restroom about an hour ago, but aside from that, she hasn't left her room. It's been blissfully quiet.

Carter should be home in a few hours.

So, I dress, waiting to shower until he *is* home, and there's an extra pair of eyes on Gabby. It's sad that she's betrayed our trust so immensely that I can't even go take a shower without Carter being here.

I'm in the kitchen, about to make a sandwich and take it in to the little girl when Carter comes walking through the front door.

It's ten thirty. I wasn't expecting him for a couple of hours yet.

The relief is instant and overwhelming.

"Hey."

He holds up a finger. "Where is she?"

"In her room."

He lets his bags drop when he stands and marches swiftly to Gabby's room.

"I have more to tell you," I say to his retreating back, but he's a man on a mission.

Gabby's going to *get it*.

Carter shuts the door firmly behind him, and the yelling starts instantly.

"What the hell is going on?"

Without remorse, I walk down the hall so I can listen in.

"I can't believe you, Gabby. This is absolutely unacceptable behavior, and you *know* it. How dare you threaten to put your hands on Nora, or anyone else. I didn't raise you to act like this."

"I just—" she begins, but he cuts her off.

"If you know what's good for you, you'll zip your mouth and listen. I had to cut an important business trip short so I could come home and deal with you because you've lost your ever-loving mind. After everything that Nora's done for you over the years, this is how you treat her?"

There's nothing for a moment as Carter undoubtedly paces around the room. I can picture it in my head, him running his hands through his hair, and Gabby biting her lip, with a scowl on her pretty face.

"I'm so disappointed in you," he says, the volume of his voice lessening, but the hardness is still in every word. "I can't believe this, Gabrielle. Who do you think you are to speak to anyone this way? To behave this way?"

"I didn't know that what I was doing was wrong."

"Bull. Shit." I cringe. That was the wrong thing to say. "I'm not stupid, thank you very much. You forget, I've been your age, you've never been mine. I know all the tricks, all the excuses."

"Sorry."

"Oh, you don't even *know* sorry yet."

I hear his footsteps approaching the door, so I scurry back to the living room. Carter comes walking out, sits on a chair, and takes a long, deep breath.

"I need a moment to calm down," he says.

"Good idea."

His eyes fly to mine. "Are you okay? I'm so sorry, Nora."

"I'm fine. I wasn't last night, but I'm better this morning. The thing is, Carter, there's more to tell you. You marched back there before I could say anything."

"There's *more*? For fuck's sake, she was in bed when I last talked to you."

"I know." I pass him her phone. "It's all on there."

I'm quiet for the next ten minutes as he scrolls through her phone, his face going from interest, to frustration, to pure rage.

"I'll fucking kill him." His voice is scarily quiet. "And then I'll kill her."

"I think threatening him will do the trick," I say, my voice brisk and business-like. "And her as well."

"She's twelve." He looks at me with helpless confusion written all over his face. "How in the ever-loving hell does this happen at twelve?"

"Oh, I'm sure this is nothing compared to some. Be thankful she never sent him nudes."

He pales now and I hear Gabby open the door of her bedroom. She walks carefully into the room, her eyes big, tears brimming.

"Dad?"

His eyes don't leave mine.

"What."

"Dad, I'm really sorry." Her lower lip is quivering now. "I didn't mean all the things I said. I'm really sorry. Honest."

"I'm not the only one you need to apologize to," he says, still not looking her in the eye. The screen of her phone is dark now, but he's staring at it, as if he's still seeing the messages.

"I'm sorry, Nora," she says softly. "I would never really hit you."

I don't say anything in reply because I'm not convinced she means it but is using this as a means to get her phone back.

"I mean it," she insists and lets a tear fall down her cheek. "I don't know why I get so mad."

"Gabby," Carter begins, his voice calmer now. "We have a lot of talking to do. We need to get to the bottom of your be-havior over the past few weeks. Has someone hurt you? Said something to you?"

"No." She looks miserable now, clamping her lips shut and shaking her head slowly. "No one hurt me."

Carter sighs and reaches out for her hand. The worst of the storm is over, but the aftermath is going to be brutal for this little girl.

"I love you more than life itself. And I'm happy to help you in any way I can, always. But I need you to meet me halfway."

She nods and wipes at her tears. "I will. I promise, I will."

"Starting today."

She nods, hope sparking in her eyes.

And here it comes.

"Can I please have my phone back?"

Carter's face goes cold again, and he sits back, watching his daughter with calculating eyes.

"You have a lot of nerve to walk in here and ask for your phone back, as if you've done nothing wrong."

"I apologized."

"Yes. But we haven't even addressed the fact that you downloaded an app that I said no to, *before* you even asked me."

Her eyes go big again, and I can see panic spreading through her.

"As if that's not enough, you've been talking to *men* on there. Giving them our address and promising to sneak them into *my* house."

"Dad—"

"No." The word cuts through anything she was about to say. "There is absolutely no excuse for any of this. You know right from wrong, Gabby, and every bit of this is wrong."

"I know." It's a whisper.

"I'll be calling this man you've been texting with."

"*Dad*—"

"And I'll explain, plainly so he can understand, that if he *ever* contacts you again, I'll ruin his life."

I feel my own eyes go wide at that statement. I've never been afraid of Carter.

The tone of his voice right now would terrify me if it were aimed at me.

"At this point, you may never get this phone back."

She swallows hard, realizing that he means business, and that she's screwed up bad.

"You can spend the rest of the day in your room."

"Fine. I'll watch TV."

Carter laughs now. "No. You've lost all privileges for the foreseeable future. I'm sure you have plenty of homework to keep you busy, since you were suspended for telling your teacher to fuck off."

She swallows hard again.

"I'm going to put this in the safe where you can't sneak it."

He stands and leaves the room, headed for the bedroom, and Gabby turns pleading eyes to me.

"I need your help. I don't know what to do. Please, help me."

"Sorry, kiddo, you've done this to yourself."

"Right. Why would you help me? You're just mad at me."

I tilt my head and watch her. "So we're back to this?"

She looks down, shame washing over her face.

"You know, your dad *brags* about you to anyone who will listen. He talks about what a good kid you are. You're hardworking, and honest, and happy. Funny. So stinkin' smart. He boasts about how trustworthy you are, and how he can depend on you to always do the right thing. That you had a bump in the road last year, but since then things have been so good."

She starts to cry in earnest now, and I want to pull her into my arms and rock her.

So I do.

"He loves you so much. You have to earn that trust back, Gabs, and only *you* can do that. Are you sure you won't just talk to him? Tell him what's bothering you?"

She shakes her head, but grips onto my shirt tightly, hugging me hard.

"I can't."

"Well, then, you need to think about things. And you need to start to make it right with your dad."

"And you," she whispers, putting hope back in my heart.

Maybe all is not lost after all.

Chapter Sixteen

~Carter~

*I*t's been a day.

Between yesterday and today, I'm convinced the gods have it out for me.

Thankfully, Gabby's been in her room all day. It's been quiet. Nora and I have alternated taking her snacks or drinks. Not because she's grounded to her room, although she should be, but because we don't want her to go hungry.

I'll punish her with lots of things, but withholding food isn't one of them.

Nora and I have also been working from the penthouse today, both deep in thought, our noses in our computers. Leaving Sacramento so abruptly lost our firm a profitable account, but I'm not sorry.

If they don't understand family emergencies, I don't want to work with them.

Thank God Quinn and Finn agreed.

"Dinner's ready," Nora says softly. "I just made an easy salad with some grilled chicken."

"That sounds great." But rather than get up to walk into the kitchen, I take her hand in mine and pull her into my lap. "Thank you."

"You're welcome." She brushes her fingers into my hair. "Are you okay?"

"Better than this morning."

She kisses my cheek. "Eating will help, too."

"I'll go get Gabby."

But first, I kiss the palm of her hand and press it to my heart, watching when her eyes go soft at the gesture.

The fact that Gabby hasn't sent her running for the hills speaks volumes.

I set Nora back on her feet and walk to Gabby's room. Without knocking, I open the door and find her on the bed, reading a magazine.

"It's time for dinner."

"I'll eat it here."

"No, you'll eat it at the table. Now."

She knows better than to roll her eyes, and she trudges behind me, as if she's being led to the guillotine.

Dramatic doesn't even begin to describe my daughter.

"Salad?" she asks with a frown, then catching herself, says, "Awesome."

"Be nice," I warn her.

We eat in silence for a few moments, then Gabby says, "This chicken is actually really good. Thanks, Nora."

"You're welcome." Nora winks at her and pops a cherry tomato in her mouth. "What have you been up to today?"

"Reading, mostly."

"I haven't had a reading day in a long time," Nora says. "That sounds really good, actually."

Gabby's quiet, frowning at her plate, and then she takes a deep breath. "I need to talk to you."

"I'll go in the bedroom—" Nora offers, but Gabby shakes her head.

"No, I need to talk to both of you."

"All right." We both turn our attention to my daughter.

"What's up, Gabs?"

"First, I really *am* sorry. I know I've been a huge pain in the a— butt." She sends me a nervous look at the almost expletive, but I don't even blink. "I guess I'm sad. And confused."

"This is a great start." Nora's smile is encouraging and soft. "Why do you think you feel that way?"

"Well, sometimes I miss my mom, and that's weird because I hardly remember her."

"Not weird," I say, reaching for Gabby's hand. "I miss her sometimes, too."

"You do?"

"Sure."

Gabby turns to Nora. "And I guess I think that if Mom knew that I love you, it would hurt her feelings."

The last few words are said in a whisper.

"Like you're betraying your mom?" Nora asks.

"Yeah. I mean, I know she's gone, and she's not coming back, but she didn't leave because she *wanted* to. She didn't have a choice. And if Dad loves someone else, and I love her, too, it's like we're forgetting Mom ever existed."

"Oh, baby." I pull her in for a big hug and feel her small body loosen as she relaxes into me. "I wish you'd told me you felt this way."

"I didn't want you to think that I don't like Nora. I do. It's just sad. I wish I knew what Mom would think about all this."

An idea grabs hold, and I pull back, smiling at my daughter. "You can. Hold on."

I hurry to the bedroom and retrieve the letter Darcy wrote to me, taking it back to the kitchen.

"Your mom wrote me a letter. Here."

"I can read it?"

"Sure, I think it'll help you feel better."

Nora and I watch her as she skims through the letter, and when she's done, she folds it and sets it on the table.

"So she knew that you would find someone else someday."

"Of course she did. Sweetheart, I was young when your mom passed away. I know it seems like I'm really old to you, but I'm not. Not really. She knew that after we'd healed, someone would come along and join our family. She wouldn't be mad that Nora's with us. She liked Nora very much, actually."

"You knew my mom?" Gabby asks Nora. "I didn't know that."

"I didn't know her superwell," Nora admits. "But yes, I'd met her several times. I worked for your dad for almost five years before she got sick."

"Oh." Gabby frowns and takes a bite of chicken. "Well, I didn't know any of this."

"Because you weren't *talking* to us and asking questions," I remind her and watch as she smiles sheepishly.

"Yeah."

"This is all new," Nora says as she pushes away her empty plate. "For all of us. And it's okay to wonder if it's the right thing, or what's going to happen in the future. Any and all of your feelings are valid. You just have to know that keeping them pent up inside you is only going to lead to what happened over the past couple of weeks, and that's no fun for anyone."

"I know," she says and nods. "I didn't want to hurt your feelings."

"*My* feelings?" Nora asks, confused.

"Yeah. Because I thought by talking about all this, it would hurt your feelings."

I sit back, watching as these two incredibly important females in my life talk it out.

"No," Nora says thoughtfully. "Conversations don't hurt my feelings. Saying things to hurt me on purpose, throwing things, threats—those are the things that hurt my feelings and make me wonder if I'm cut out for this at all."

What? I stare at her in shock.

"What do you mean?" I ask, keeping my voice calm.

"Well, parenting is hard, obviously. And last night, I couldn't help but wonder if I'm the person you both need to be in your lives. Gabby's been so unhappy, I thought maybe I'm just not a good fit here."

"It's not you," Gabby rushes to assure her. "Honest, it's all my fault."

And mine, for not encouraging and reinforcing strongly enough that Nora's *exactly* the right person to be in our lives.

I plan to fix that, immediately.

"Thanks for saying so," Nora says. "Love you, kiddo."

"I love you, too." Gabby hurries over to hug Nora tight. "I'm sorry I'm a jerk."

"You're not always a jerk."

THE GABBY HURRICANE seems to have passed. It's been several days since her apology, and for the most part, things have gone back to normal.

It's a huge weight that's been lifted from my shoulders. I missed my good-natured, happy girl.

I also made some calls this morning. First, to Jacob's Ladder. I informed him that he'd be facing criminal charges regarding a minor, and then I contacted the police. It seems his Instagram handle isn't new to them, but I can do my best to make sure he doesn't target any more young girls.

It's the end of a successful workday. Nora and I have passed the Dickinson file back and forth throughout the day, flirting and being silly.

It's fun to play with her.

In fact, I think I'll play with her some more.

I pick up the phone and call for her to come into my office.

"Close and lock the door, please." Nora turns to me in surprise but follows my orders and then saunters over to my desk, walking on those heels with the red bows on them.

They're my favorite.

I can't resist her when she wears them.

And she knows it.

"You rang?" she asks primly, folding her hands at her waist.

"I did. Come here, please." I crook my finger and feel my lips twitch as she raises a brow and slowly walks around my desk, then plants her feet two feet in front of me.

"Yes?"

"I have some things to tell you."

"I'm all ears."

I grin and tug her closer, until she's standing between my legs, and press my ear to her belly.

Her hands dive into my hair and I turn my face to her, kissing her stomach over her clothes.

"You're so sassy," I murmur before tugging her blouse out of her skirt and standing so I can lift it over her head, then toss it on the floor. Her bra goes next.

"We're at work," she reminds me, but there's no heat in her words.

"So we are."

"Rule number one—"

"No longer exists." I pull her nipple into my mouth and suck. Hard. Then pay the same respects to the other side. I boost her onto my desk.

"I'm on your briefs."

My lips, on hers now, tip up into a grin. "I love it when you talk dirty, darling."

She laughs now, a full-on laugh that's as contagious as it is sexy. I slide my fingers up her thigh, under her skirt. The laugh subsides as I push under the elastic of her panties and just rub back and forth over her folds.

"Oh God."

"Does that feel good?"

"Oh yeah." Her head falls back as she bites her lip. "Don't stop petting me there."

"Petting?" I lean in and lap at her nipple, slip my finger inside her, and revel at how gorgeous she is as she falls apart, crying out my name and squeezing my finger. "There you go. That's it."

"Holy shit."

I unfasten my pants, and before she has a chance to recover, slide inside her, balls deep. She cries out again, reaching for me as I begin to move, fucking her on my desk, not caring in the least who might hear us outside of my office.

She's holding on for dear life, those brown eyes on fire as I pound into her, almost brutally.

"Jesus, you destroy me." I press my face to her shoulder as I come, undone by her.

"Not sorry." She kisses my cheek and squeezes my ass for good measure. "Not sorry at all."

I slip out of her, stand her on her feet, and turn her. With my hand pressed between her shoulder blades, I gently push her facedown on the desk.

"Again?" she asks in surprise as I fill her once more, from behind this time, and smack her ass.

"Again."

I can't get enough of her. I feel like an animal, unable to stop myself from wanting to mate with her.

I'm out of control.

I last much longer this time and reach around to fiddle with her nipples, her clit, as we ride our way toward release.

This orgasm is loud and primal, tearing through me and leaving me decimated.

"Whoa," she whispers. "That was . . . I don't even know."

"Did I hurt you?"

"You didn't do anything I didn't want you to."

I smile and press my lips to her spine. "That's the right answer, darling."

I NEED TO propose to her. I *want* to ask her to marry me. This brutal week has taught me one thing, and that's that I don't want to carry on through this life without her.

When Darcy died, I was convinced that I'd never move on.

I loved her completely, and our marriage, while not easy, was a good one. We shared a lot of wonderful memories, and I'll always be grateful to her for sharing her life with me and giving me Gabby.

My love for Darcy was never in question.

And when she died, I didn't think it was a hole that could be filled.

But it's true what they say: time heals all wounds.

Life moves forward, and while I'll never forget her, just like she said in her letter, it's time for me to embrace the fact that I've fallen in love with Nora and start to plan our future.

There's no one else I want by my side.

And it may be fast, but damn it, I'm a man who knows his own mind, and I'm ready to marry her.

It's really that simple.

Nora's in the shower, getting ready for bed, and I'm sitting under the covers, staring at the single stone engagement ring I chose for her weeks ago.

I carry it with me, always ready to propose because I just never know when the right moment will reveal itself. Of course, with the crazy week we just had, there was literally *no* romantic moment to ask Nora to be my bride.

Not when I had a temperamental preteen to deal with.

But that storm has passed, and we're back on course.

Now, I just need to decide when and where to ask her. It shouldn't be in bed. It should be somewhere romantic, with flowers and candles and soft music.

Shit, I should ask her parents first.

I swallow hard, remembering how Nora's relationship with her parents is as tenuous as mine, but it's the right thing to do.

I'll call them tomorrow, get their blessing, and then propose this weekend.

I nod, happy with the plan; I slip the ring into its box and tuck it away in my nightstand. Nora snaps the shower off, and I reach for my iPad, ready to do some reading before sleep.

I hear her in the bathroom, opening and shutting drawers, going about her ritual.

It's become our nightly routine, and I would be lying if I said I didn't enjoy it.

I've just sunk into an article on the chemicals they put in coffee creamer when Nora walks into the bedroom. I glance up, and do a double take when I see the concerned expression on her lovely face.

"What's the matter?"

"I don't know. It might be nothing."

"What might be nothing?"

"I don't want to freak you out."

"You're freaking me out anyway." I set the iPad aside and sit forward as she sits on the edge of the bed. "Seriously, talk to me."

"Okay. Feel this." She takes my hand and rubs it over the underside of her breast, back and forth. I can feel something firm, about the size of a pea.

About the size of a pea.

Fuck me.

"Do you feel it?" she asks.

"I do." I sit back and try to keep my emotions under control. I want to scoop her up and take her immediately to the emergency room and demand a mammogram on the spot.

I want to scream.

Hell, I want to curl up and cry like a damn baby.

But I don't do any of those things.

"It could be nothing, right?" She bites her lip and turns pleading eyes to mine. "It's probably not cancer."

Cancer. I fucking hate that word. The mention of it sets my pulse racing and fills me with absolute terror. If it *is* cancer, I don't know what I'll do. I can't go through it again. I can't lose another woman that I love more than anything in the world.

"Probably not."

I hear the coldness in my voice and cringe when she turns confused eyes on me.

"I'm sure it's nothing." There, that sounds better. She crawls up onto the bed and lays her head in my lap. Because it's what she needs, I brush my fingers through the soft strands.

"I'm healthy," she says, as if she's trying to convince us both. "I'm young, and I take care of myself. Sure, I like cake as much as the next girl, and I have a few extra pounds that I carry around, but for the most part, I'm healthy. The only pills I take are Advil for the occasional headache."

"You're incredibly healthy," I agree, reminding us both. And God wouldn't do this to me twice.

Would he?

"It's probably just a cyst," she continues. "I think my mom has had a few cysts, and my doctor once told me that I have fibrous breasts, whatever that means."

I tune her out now, unable to hear her over the roaring in my ears.

A lump.

Cancer.

My God, what will Gabby and I do if we lose her? Am I being melodramatic?

Maybe.

Maybe Gabby gets the drama from me.

But I've been here before, and it's terrifying. Darcy and I had the same conversation.

Young and healthy.

Probably nothing.

It could be a thousand things, no need to jump to conclusions.

Everything's going to be just fine.

Almost verbatim, it's a conversation that I've had before, and my world fell apart.

How could it be happening again?

Chapter Seventeen

~Nora~

"What's wrong with you?"

I'm riding in the back of a cab with Christopher, on our way to my doctor appointment to have my breast checked.

"Oh, you know, lump in my breast." I stare at him like he's ridiculous. "Nothing to worry about here."

"No, I get that part, that's why I'm here. But I sense more than fear. I sense anger in you."

"Well, Yoda, you're right. I'm good and pissed off."

He wraps an arm around my shoulders. "Talk to me."

I take a long, deep breath. "Ever since last night when I asked Carter to feel my breast, to make sure I'm not crazy, he's gone cold on me. I told him about my appointment today this morning at the office and asked him to come with me. He said he didn't have time."

"Maybe he didn't."

"I *know* his schedule. Hell, I *make* his schedule. I know he could have taken a couple of hours to go to the doctor with me. He's just shut down on me, and I can't figure it out. Everything was going so well after Gabby's meltdown, and then *poof.* Cold."

"So I *wasn't* your first choice to go to the doctor with you?"

I stare at him. Christopher smiles and tightens the arm around me in a hug. "Kidding. I'm here for the comic relief, after all."

"Why is my man being a colossal jerk?"

"Didn't you tell me his wife died of cancer?"

"Yeah, about five years ago."

"And now you're worried that you could have breast *cancer.*"

I blink, then lean into Christopher when the cabbie takes a left turn a little too fast.

"You're right. He must be scared."

"There you go."

I'm feeling sick to my stomach by the time we pull up to the clinic, and I chalk it up to car sickness and nerves.

I'm so nervous.

But Christopher takes my hand as we walk inside, and I check in with the receptionist. I pretend to read a *People* magazine as we wait, but my name is finally called.

"I'll stay here," Chris says, but I shake my head.

"Like hell you will. You're with me."

He rolls his eyes but follows me. The nurse leads me to a scale, where I learn I've gained ten pounds since last year.

Lovely. This day just gets better and better.

Once we're in a room, she takes all my vitals, asks questions, and then leaves Christopher and me alone to wait for the doctor.

"She tried to take my arm off with the blood pressure cuff." I rub my upper arm with a scowl before stripping out of my shirt and bra to put the gown on, open side to the front, per the nurse's instructions. "I hate that part."

"It was high, too." Christopher frowns at the gown. "That green's not really your color."

"Well, yeah. I'm a little nervous here." I tie the front and sit next to him again.

"No need, sugar. It's all going to be just fine. I'm always right about these things."

"You're full of shit." But he's made me laugh, loosening my stomach muscles just a bit. No matter what, I can depend on Christopher to be by my side, to hold my hand and make me smile.

He's the best friend ever.

"Good afternoon." Dr. Gonzales bustles into the room. She's a petite woman, with shiny black hair, brown eyes, and thick black glasses.

"Hello," I reply.

"So you think you've found a lump?"

"Yes. I don't remember it being there before."

"Let's have a look." She smiles kindly and gestures for me to hop up on the table. "Lie back for me. I'm going to feel your breasts."

She lifts my right arm over my head, exposes that breast and starts to poke around. I wince a bit at the tenderness.

"Nothing here," she says, covering me back up before moving to the left breast. She goes through the same motions, and when she gets to the underside, pauses.

"That's it," I whisper, watching her face. Her eyes narrow. "What is it?"

"Are you tender?"

"Yeah." I wince again when she moves her fingers up over my nipple. "Pretty tender."

"Are you about to start your period?"

I pause, thinking. "Actually, yes. I should be. It's been a while."

"Hmm." She finishes up, covers me, and backs away. "You can sit up."

"Is it a tumor?"

"No," she replies immediately, and I am instantly filled with relief. "Our breasts change as we age, and even monthly during our cycle. You have fibrous breasts. I want to run a urine sample real quick while you're here."

She passes me a plastic cup and gives me directions around the corner and promises to meet me back in the room soon.

Once I've done my business and returned to the room, Christopher and I wait only about five minutes before Dr. Gonzales returns.

"It's what I suspected," she says with a smile. "Breasts can also change, develop little benign cysts, when you're pregnant."

I frown. "What does that have to do with me?"

"Oh, honey." Christopher pats my knee and the doctor smiles again.

"You're pregnant. You're going to be parents."

"Whoa, don't look at me." Chris throws his hands up in surrender. "I didn't do this. I don't touch girls like that." He turns to me. "Her gaydar is broken."

"Well, regardless of who the father is, you're definitely pregnant." She's making notes in her computer. "We'll need to discuss when your last period was, so we can ballpark your due date."

"But my boyfriend had a vasectomy years ago. We don't use other birth control because it's a monogamous relationship."

She nods and purses her lips. "I've seen cases, and read of others, where the vasectomy didn't take."

"*Didn't take?*" I stare at her, dumbfounded. "The whole job of the vasectomy is to *take*."

"It's rare, but it happens. Before you leave, we'll schedule you for your first prenatal visit. In the meantime, no alcohol or smoking. If you need a prescription medication, it has to be approved by me."

I nod, trying to listen to her, but my head is buzzing.

I'm pregnant.

I'm going to have a baby.

Holy shit.

Once we're in another cab, Christopher sighs. "Are you okay?"

"I don't know. I was *not* expecting this."

"I know. But are you okay?"

"I guess. I mean, it'll all work out, right? Carter's a great dad, and the Cavanaugh family is amazing. We'll have support from them. Gabby'll be a great big sister."

"That's all true," he says and pats my knee. "After he gets over the initial shock, Carter will be happy."

"Well, I hope so. Obviously he didn't plan to have more children, but babies are a wonderful thing."

"Totally," Christopher agrees. The cab pulls up to my office building. "This is your stop. If you need me later, just call. I have the rest of the day free."

"Thank you." I lean in and kiss his cheek. "You're the best friend a girl could have."

"You're making me blush. Good luck, sugar."

I climb out of the cab and make my way inside. The closer I get to my desk, the more nervous I get. I want Carter to be happy. Excited, even.

Frankly, I don't see why he wouldn't be.

I press my hand to my stomach in the elevator and grin. *I'm going to have a baby.*

When I return to my desk, I see that Carter's in a meeting. I've never been patient. Waiting around, especially with news like this, is painful.

But finally, after about thirty minutes, Carter walks out of the elevator toward his office. He doesn't even glance my way. His face is completely blank as he walks past my desk.

We're about to have a conversation about him being a dick. I told him before, the silent treatment pisses me off.

Without being invited, I follow him into the office and shut the door smartly behind me, getting his attention.

"Would you like to hear how my appointment went?"

He raises a brow expectantly, but when I wait for him to respond to my question, he simply says, "If you'd like to share, please go ahead."

I walk toward him and cock my head to the side. "Well, I see where Gabby gets her shitty attitude. This is not unlike what I got from your daughter just a few days ago."

Carter blows out a breath and rubs his hand down his face. "I apologize. You're right. Please tell me what the doctor said."

"I don't have cancer."

Every muscle in his body slumps with the news. He covers his eyes and sighs in relief. "Thank God."

He was scared. The coldness, the distance, was out of fear.

"I was terrified," he admits now.

"I know. Me, too. But it's definitely *not* cancer." I sit across from him. "She said that as we age, the texture of the tissue can change, particularly when a woman is pregnant."

His eyes, his entire face, goes blank once again.

He says nothing for ten long seconds.

"Carter? Did you hear me?"

"I heard."

"I mean, I know this was *not* planned, but—"

"Whose is it?"

The words echo in the space between us, and my eyes narrow on him—this man I've fallen in love with and trusted with my heart.

He raises his brows again, expecting an answer. I'm shaking in rage as I slowly stand from my chair, brace my hands on the desk as I lean over, and say in no uncertain terms, "You can go fuck yourself."

With that, I walk out of his office, slamming the door behind me. Childish? Sure, but it felt damn good. I'm doing my best to keep tears at bay as I gather my things and hurry to the elevator.

I need to get the hell out of here.

"Hey, Nora." Sienna joins me at the elevator, and when she sees my face, she frowns. "What's wrong?"

I shake my head. I just need to be alone. I need to get the hell out of here and be alone. I'm about to break apart, and I refuse to do it here.

"Nora, talk to me," she tries again and lays her hand on my shoulder. "You're scaring me. Are you okay? Are you hurt?"

The elevator arrives, and as the doors open, I shake my head and say, "If you want answers, go ask Carter. I have to go."

I step in and when the doors close, I breathe a sigh of relief.

But I'm not in here alone. No, that would be too easy.

So I keep breathing. In through the nose, out through the mouth. Don't think about the fact that the man you love just called you a whore. Hold it together.

"Hello, Nora."

Motherfucker.

"Mary" is all I say and I watch the numbers ping as we pass each floor.

"Gee, you look upset. Are you okay? Did Carter break up with you?" She clicks her tongue. "That's why no-frat policies exist, you know. So things like *this* don't happen. So someone doesn't march through the place with a red, blotchy face, making a fool of herself."

Enough.

I round on her and trap her in the corner of the elevator.

"If you touch me, I'll press charges," she threatens, but she's scared.

And right now, she should be.

"I've had enough of your shit. You can take your jealous, pathetic opinions and shove them up your ass, Mary."

"I'll recommend you be terminated," she sputters. "There are cameras in here. You're threatening me."

"No need." I back away as the door dings. "I quit. Effective right now."

"Good! You were toxic here—"

"Oh, just fuck right off," I say, not even looking back as I walk off the elevator and raise my hand, flipping her off.

I hurry home. I want to be in my space, where I feel safe. But once I get there, all I see is Gabby everywhere. She helped me decorate every room of this apartment. She stayed with me here.

Carter made love to me here.

I can't be here, after all. So I call Christopher.

"Hey, sugar."

"I'm coming up, so I hope you're home."

"I am," he confirms. I hang up and hurry up the stairs, not even bothering to wait for the elevator. When I reach his apartment, the door is open and he's standing there, his arms open and waiting to give me a massive hug.

"I hate men," I mumble into his chest. "No offense."

"None taken." With his arms still around me, he moves us inside and shuts the door, then steers me to the couch, and I stare at him. "So he's not happy?"

I shake my head and let the tears come now. "No. He's not happy."

"What did he say?"

"He asked me who the father is."

Chris's eyes bulge, his jaw drops. And then he goes red.

"I do believe I'm going to kick his ass," he says. "Who the fuck does he think he is to say something like that?"

"It was a shock." It's a weak excuse, and we both know it. "That's all I got."

"It's not good enough," he says quietly. "I'm so damn sorry, Nora. What are you going to do?"

"What do you mean?"

He rubs his nose, leans his head side to side, as if the thought in his head is uncomfortable, but finally he says, "I mean, are you going to keep it? Do you need me to take you to a clinic, or—"

"Oh, no. I'm not going to abort it, if that's what you're asking. Carter can be a dick all day long, but that doesn't mean that I'll do anything but love this baby." I cover my stomach. "I can raise it alone. I quit my job just now, but I'll find another."

"You quit?"

"Yeah, I ran into the bitch Mary in the elevator, and she works in HR."

"The one that's been harassing you?"

I nod.

"I hope you punched her."

"I wanted to, but then she would have pressed charges, and if you think green isn't my color, well, orange *definitely* isn't my color, and I don't want to give birth in a prison."

"They would take you to a hospital to have the baby. At least, that's what happens in the movies."

"Well, that's something then, isn't it."

We stare at each other for a moment, and then bust up laughing.

"It's not funny," I say as I try to catch my breath.

"The idea of you giving birth in prison is pretty funny." He reaches over to brush a tear off my cheek. "But it won't come to that. So you told Mary you quit?"

"Yeah. After I told Carter to go fuck himself."

"That's my girl."

I lie on the couch and rest my head in his lap. He immediately runs his fingers through my hair.

"I'm sorry it's come to this, sugar. Maybe Carter will see the error of his ways and he'll come begging for forgiveness."

"How do I forgive this?" I turn to my back so I can look up into his face. "When I told him I don't have cancer, he literally slumped in his chair. He was cold because he was scared, and I immediately forgave him for that in my head. I can understand fear, especially after losing his wife the way he did. It makes sense to me.

"But then, in the next breath, to accuse me of cheating on him? Come on. I *divorced* a man for cheating on me, and he knows that. It's the worst sin you can accuse me of. And if he thinks I'm capable of screwing around with some other man when I'm also having a relationship with *him*, well, he doesn't know me very well, does he?"

"No," Christopher says softly. "He obviously doesn't."

"I just don't know how we bounce back from this. I don't know what he could possibly say that would make sense to me. Because even if he says it was a shock because he'd had the vasectomy, which again I would understand if he'd just said that in the first place, he called me a whore. That's what it boils down to."

"You're getting yourself worked up again, and you're over-thinking it." He lays his hand over my forehead. It feels cool against my hot skin. "That's not good for you *or* the baby."

"Are you going to be bossy like this the whole time I'm pregnant?"

"Someone has to look out for you," he says with a smile. "So, yeah, I am. I'm also going to fix you a bowl of chicken soup and a grilled cheese sandwich because I doubt you've eaten today, and you need to eat for the baby."

"You're a mother hen," I accuse. But he slips out from under me and walks into the kitchen. I listen to him bustle about, taking care of me.

I needed Carter to take care of me like this. To jump in and ask me if I'm okay, to insist I eat, to ask when we go to the doctor next.

I needed him.

And he failed miserably.

I wipe a tear as it falls down my cheek and call myself four kinds of a fool for letting him hurt me this way.

But it does hurt.

More than I ever thought possible.

"How many sandwiches do you want?" Christopher asks from the kitchen.

"Just one."

"I'm making you two," he warns. "You don't have to eat it all, but it'll be there if you want it."

"Thank you. For everything today, not just this. I know you took the day off work to help me out, and I appreciate it."

"I love you," he says simply. "If you need me, I'm here."

And that's exactly, *exactly* what I needed from Carter. But now I know where I stand. I know I'll never hear those words from him.

Chapter Eighteen

~Carter~

I don't know what the fuck just happened.

I'm standing at the window, hands shoved in my pockets and the echo of the door slamming still in the air around me.

She's pregnant.

And it's not medically possible that it's mine.

"Jesus." I rub my hand over my neck. I thought I knew her. I thought what we had was solid and true.

How did I judge the whole situation so damn poorly?

"You."

I turn and watch as Sienna marches into my office, her eyes shooting daggers at me.

"I don't have time to—"

"You'll make the goddamn time," she interrupts and points to my chair. "Sit."

I look at Finn and Quinn, who followed her into the room, rushing to keep up with her.

Sienna's a little thing, but she moves fast when she wants to and she can be damn intimidating.

It's why she's such a good attorney.

Finn shrugs and Quinn just sits on the couch across the room, and I find myself following Sienna's direction, lowering slowly into my own chair.

"You're being charged with hurting someone I care about," she says, pacing in front of my desk. "What's your plea?"

"Guilty," I mutter. "But I don't have time to talk to you—"

"You won't speak unless you're answering my questions," she says and I glance at the guys again, but again, they shrug.

"Now, tell the court what happened last night."

I frown. "Last night?"

"That's what I said."

"Objection," Finn says, coming to my defense. Quinn winces. "What does that have to do with the matter at hand?"

"I'm laying groundwork," Sienna replies coolly and turns her gaze to me. "Answer me, please."

"Nora found what she believed to be a lump in her breast."

All their eyes go round, and Finn's face pales.

"Fuck," Quinn mutters.

"And I was an asshole about it," I volunteer. "It scared me, okay? It was déjà vu. Suddenly the woman I love is making me feel for a lump, which I can also *feel*, and it fucking terrified me."

"Understandable," Sienna says softly. "But through the fear, you reassured her, right? You hugged her and said everything would be okay. You made her feel treasured."

"Objection," Quinn says. "Leading the witness."

"I clammed up and barely spoke to her," I admit. "She asked me to go to her appointment with her this afternoon, and I told her I was too busy."

"Jesus, you *are* a jerk," Sienna says with a roll of the eyes. "Then what happened?"

"She returned from the appointment and told me that it isn't cancer."

"Thank God," Finn says. "So everything's fine then, right?"

"It wasn't when I ran into Nora at the elevator," Sienna says, her eyes narrowed and focused on mine. "Nothing seemed to be okay at all."

"What did she say?" I ask, standing. "Was she crying?"

"I'm asking the questions."

"Fuck that. Tell me if she was okay."

"Of course she wasn't okay, you idiot. She was upset, but she wasn't crying. Yet."

I cringe and pace to the window again.

"If she doesn't have cancer, why was she upset?" Quinn asks.

"She's pregnant," I reply, the words dry cardboard on my tongue.

"Whoa." I turn at Finn's voice. "Well, it's a surprise, but we all love kids."

"I asked her who the father is."

All three pairs of eyes stare at me as if I just told them my name is Sylvia.

"I'm so glad you don't share DNA with this man," Sienna says to Quinn, who doesn't take his eyes off mine. "What the hell do you mean?" Sienna asks. "Of course it's yours."

"I had a vasectomy years ago, when Darcy was alive." I sit in my chair, suddenly feeling bone-tired. God, I'm exhausted. "It's impossible that it's mine."

"Are you sure?" Quinn asks. "Did you go in for your follow-up appointment after the procedure to make sure the swimmers were gone?"

I frown at my brother-in-law. "Of course I did." I blink, thinking back. "I mean, I think."

"You *think*," Finn says.

Sienna stomps to my desk, picks up the phone, and thrusts it under my nose.

"Call the clinic right now and ask them."

"Jesus, you're pushy."

"You haven't seen pushy yet, pal. Call the damn clinic."

"I could fire you."

"Go ahead." She lifts her chin, and I find myself doing as she demands, dialing the number to my doctor's office.

"Manhattan Wellness Clinic, this is Hilary, how can I help you?"

"Hilary, this is Carter Shaw. Is there any way you can tell me if I had an appointment about five years ago?"

"Sure, our records go back that far. I'll have a record here of all appointments you've made. What kind of visit would it have been?"

"I had a vasectomy in the summer of 2015. Do you see if I ever had a follow-up appointment?"

"Let me check," she murmurs, and then says, "I see it. Yep, you did have a follow-up six weeks after the procedure."

I nod, victorious that everything with me is as it should be, and the baby most certainly is *not* mine.

"But you were a no-show," she continues, and I stop cold.

"Excuse me?"

"I show here that you no-showed for the appointment, and you never rescheduled. In fact, we didn't see you until two years later, when you came in for a yearly physical."

"What was the date of the no-show?"

"July twenty-sixth."

I sigh and rub my hand down my face.

"I see. Thank you, Hilary."

"Sure thing. Have a good day." She hangs up and I stare blankly at Finn, Quinn, and Sienna.

"Well, shit."

"So, you did not, in fact, ever follow up to make sure the procedure was successful," Sienna says, all business once again.

"It would seem I didn't. Because that was the day Darcy died, and I was a little preoccupied."

"Oh," Sienna says and sends me a sympathetic glance. "I'm sorry, Carter. I really am."

"Yeah, me, too."

"So, to summarize," Finn says, rubbing his hands briskly up and down his thighs as he thinks the situation over. "Your swimmers are alive and well. Nora's pregnant. You accused her of fucking around on you, and she left, upset."

"Basically, you're a dumbass," Quinn adds with a nod.

I can't even argue with him. I *am* a dumbass.

"Yeah."

Sienna's worrying her bottom lip between her thumb and forefinger, lost in thought.

"You have to fix it."

"Good luck," Finn mutters.

"He can still fix it," Sienna says to Finn, nodding slowly. "You'll need to grovel. Apologize like your life depends on it."

"Because it does," I mutter. "I was cruel."

"So much groveling," Sienna repeats. "And you need to *talk*. Explain what was going through your head. I mean, I assume she knows you had the vasectomy."

"I told her," I confirm. "It was our only form of birth control."

"Then if you talk to her and explain everything, you might have a chance of making it right. I mean, you love each other. People in love screw up, but then they make it right."

I frown.

"You do love her, don't you?"

"Of course." I swallow hard. *Jesus, I love her so much.*

"Then my money's on you."

"Mine's not," Finn says cheerfully. "But you're going to be a daddy again, and that's something to celebrate."

"A baby." I shake my head in disbelief. "I'm starting all over again after forty. I'm going to be an old dad."

"Not that old," Quinn says. "You'll be fine."

"First things first," Sienna says. "You need to get to Nora and make things right. Because coming from a woman's point of view, you fucked up big-time, Carter, and this isn't going to be easy."

"I know. So what do I do?"

"Find her. Be honest with her."

"Take flowers," Quinn adds. "And probably chocolate."

"Jewelry," Finn says, shaking his head. "This is a job for precious gems. Gold. Hit up Tiffany's around the corner on your way out."

I already have that covered.

"I'm going," I say. Before I can get to the door, a woman pops her head in.

"Mr. Shaw?"

"What."

She blinks at my harsh tone. "Um, I'm Mary, from HR. With Nora quitting so abruptly, I've found someone to fill in for her until we can—"

"She *quit*?"

A smile spreads on Mary's face, and now I see it. The reason why Nora doesn't trust her.

"Piece of work," Sienna mutters behind me.

"Don't worry about Nora," I say to Mary. "I have it covered. And you can clean out your desk and go home. You're fired."

"What?" She pales. "You can't fire me. I didn't do anything wrong."

"I can do whatever the hell I want because *I own this company*."

"I'll sue for wrongful termination."

All four of us chuckle.

"You do realize you just threatened a room full of attorneys," Finn says. "You heard him. Gather your things and go."

She glares, then stomps away.

"That was a long time coming," Sienna says. "That woman has had it out for Nora for months. Good riddance."

"It's about time I protect my woman," I say, my voice grim. "I'm embarrassed to admit I haven't been good at that up to now."

"You can make it right," Sienna assures me.

"Maybe just give her cash," Quinn says thoughtfully. "I wonder if a hundred grand would be enough?"

"I'll give her whatever she wants, if she'll just forgive me."

"Go get her, tiger," Sienna says, giving me the thumbs-up. "You've got this."

I DON'T HAVE this.

I mean, I do have the ring in my pocket, a huge bouquet of white roses, and Nora's favorite cupcakes from Magnolia for good measure.

I'm loaded down with offerings of apology.

Now I just have to make her see that I didn't mean anything that I said. I have to make it right.

I pound on her door and then press my ear to it, listening. I don't hear any movement. Where else would she go? She's not at my place, I was just there to retrieve the ring.

I bang again and wait.

Nothing.

Finally, I dial her number and continue to bang on the door.

"I don't want to talk to you," she says into my ear.

"Open the door, Nora. Please."

"I'm not home, you big jerk. Why do you want to talk to a cheater like me, anyway?"

I wince. "I deserved that. Please, darling. Please let me make this right. I need to talk to you."

She hangs up without another word, and I slump against the door in defeat.

She's not here, and she doesn't want to hear what I have to say.

I'm screwed.

The elevator doors open at the end of the hall, and she comes marching out, her mouth set in a grim line and her brown eyes narrowed, not looking directly at me.

When she reaches the door, she pushes me out of the way and walks right in.

"The door wasn't locked? Nora, you shouldn't leave your apartment unlocked. You don't know what kind of whack job might just walk right in."

"Like you?" she counters, leaning on the kitchen island. "Are you really going to lecture me about *anything* right now?"

I take a deep breath and slowly let it out. "No. You're right. I brought these for you."

I hold the cupcakes and flowers out for her, but she just spares them a glance, looks up at me, and doesn't walk forward to take them.

Okay.

I set everything on the countertop and pace away, shoving my fingers through my hair in agitation.

"I fucked up."

"Big-time," she agrees.

"I know. I was wrong."

"Which time?"

"Excuse me?"

She walks around the island, toward me. "Which time, exactly, were you wrong? Was it last night, when I was worried and I went to you, looking for support? Or this morning, when I asked you to go to the doctor with me, and you *lied* to me about your schedule being full? *I'm* the one who fills your schedule, Carter. I know you had the time."

"Well, I—"

"I'm not done." She digs her pointy little finger into my chest. "Christopher went with me, by the way. Not that you care."

"I care."

She shakes her head and walks away. "Or were you wrong when I got back to the office, and you didn't even fucking *ask me* how the appointment went? I had to basically beg you to care."

Jesus, I'm so ashamed.

"I had my walls up because I was scared."

"I get it," she says with a nod. "I know what you've been

through in the past, and I understand. I really do. In that moment in your office, when you finally apologized for being cold, and admitted to being afraid, I totally forgave you for the previous eighteen hours, without a problem."

"You did?"

"Of course." She throws her hands up in frustration and paces away. "I'm not stupid, Carter. You lost your *wife* to cancer, of course you were scared. We both have some baggage, and it's going to rear its ugly head once in a while."

She's right. We do. And no matter how much we think we've moved on, there will be bad moments from time to time.

"Here's what I don't forgive," she continues and I brace myself because I'm quite sure what's coming is going to knock me on my ass. "I told you I'm pregnant."

Her eyes fill with tears, and I move to hold her, but she scurries away, out of my reach.

"Damn it, Nora."

"I told you I'm pregnant, and rather than ask me questions like 'How is this possible?' or 'Are you sure?,' you asked me who the father is."

A tear slips down her cheek.

"You accused me of something that I hate so much, something that ruined my first marriage. How could you possibly think after the past weeks together that I would ever want anyone else? And not only that, how in the bloody hell could I find time to fuck someone else? I'm with you twenty-four/seven, for God's sake!"

"I know. Nora, you're completely right. I'm a colossal dick, and I was so thrown, I just reacted without thinking."

"I would never do that to you," she whispers. "Not just because I think cheaters are horrible, but because I know what that feels like. I know how much that hurts. I would *never* make you feel like that."

"I know." It's all I can say.

"And in return, you made me feel like a whore."

"Christ." I pace away from her, and then back again. "I never meant that, Nora. You mean too much to me to ever intentionally hurt you like that."

"The words came out of your mouth." She angrily swipes away a tear.

"I wish I could take them back. With all my heart, I wish I could go back and do it all differently. Starting with last night."

"Me, too."

"I can't do that." I hold my hands out at my sides. "I can only apologize, with everything I am, for ever making you feel like I don't care. And for hurting you so deeply."

"The trust is cracked a bit here, Carter. I've never seen this kind of behavior from you, and it scared me."

"I'll earn it all back," I promise as I walk to her. She doesn't push away this time as I pull her into my arms and hug her closely. "I know it'll take some time, but I'll make it up to you."

"So you're not freaked out about the baby?"

"Oh, I'm a little freaked out." I kiss her head and take a deep breath, pulling the scent of her in. "First, I was confused. I *did* have the vasectomy, like I told you. But I called the office, and I never made it to the follow-up appointment, where they make sure the procedure was a success."

Her head whips up. "Why ever not?"

"Because Darcy died the day of that appointment, and I missed it. It just slipped my mind, with everything happening."

"Of course," she whispers. "Well, I guess it makes sense then."

"Yeah." I brush my hand down her hair. "How do you feel?"

"Tired."

"Is that from me being a jerk, or the baby?"

"Maybe both," she admits with a smile.

"Mary came to my office," I say and watch as the smile slides from her face. "She said you quit."

"Yeah. I might have also cornered her in the elevator and told her to fuck off."

"You've had a busy day of telling people to fuck off, darling."

"If my memory serves, I told you to go fuck yourself."

I kiss her forehead. "So you did. Charming."

"You deserved it."

"And more."

"What did Mary say?"

"Just that you'd quit, and she found me a temp. I told her to let me take care of things regarding you, and she could go ahead and leave. I fired her."

She looks up in surprise again. "You *fired* her?"

"She's made enough waves in the office. We don't need a troublemaker at Cavanaugh Cavanaugh and Shaw."

"I don't like her," Nora admits.

"Well, she's gone. Now, I'm so glad we've started to mend things here, because we're about to be very busy."

"What are you talking about?"

I take the ring out of my pocket and place it on her ring finger.

"We have a wedding to plan."

"Like hell we do."

Chapter Nineteen

~Nora~

I yank the ring off my finger, shove it into Carter's chest, and pull away from him.

"What are you doing?" He's scowling at me, confusion written all over his face. "Of course we're getting married."

"Of course we're getting married." I look up to the ceiling, begging for strength from any god that's listening. Actually, no. It's patience I need. Because if God gives me strength, I'll strangle him.

"I don't know if you've heard," I begin as I pace my living room. "But it's 2020. Not 1972. I am perfectly capable of being a single parent. There's no law that states we have to get married. I'm not an attorney, and even *I* know that."

He's blinking fast. The ring is still gripped in his fingers.

"Do you think I'm proposing because you're *pregnant*?"

"Aren't you?" I challenge and prop my hands on my hips.

"Well, it's part of it, but no. Of course not."

"Why are you then?" I lift my chin and promise myself I won't cry. I will *not* cry. "I won't get married out of obligation or convenience ever again, Carter. I've been there, done that, and it won't happen again. Not for me."

"Jesus, Nora, that's not what this is."

I just stare at him, until he shoves the ring back in his pocket and stomps away, rubbing his hand over his mouth in agitation.

"Why are women so damn frustrating, that's what I want to know," he mutters. "I don't know what it is you want me to say. What do you want from me?"

"I want you to love me, you moron!" My hands fist. I might clock him one after all. "You've never said you *love* me. And that's the only reason to get married."

He's staring at me like I just blew an apple out of my nose.

"What are you even talking about? Of course I've told you I love you."

"Uh, no. Pretty sure I would have remembered that."

"What do you think I'm saying every time I kiss your hand and place it on my heart?"

Now it's my turn to stare. We're doing a lot of staring.

"Well, since I'm not a freaking mind reader, I thought it was a sweet gesture."

"I can't believe this."

"You've never said the *words*, Carter."

"My God. The Florida condo, the time with my family—"

"Were all wonderful," I confirm with a nod. "But are not words of love."

"You've never said it, either," he says, crossing his arms over his chest.

"You're right. I haven't. Because I was afraid to tell you how deeply I'd fallen in love with you, only to have you pat me on the head and say *thank you*. Do you have any idea how completely embarrassing that would be?"

"Never would have happened."

"I didn't *know* that."

"We fucked this up," he mutters, shaking his head in disgust. "And rather than argue over it, I'd like to fix it."

"That would be ideal, yes. Because I'm carrying *your* baby, and despite wanting to toss you out that window to the concrete below, I love you to distraction." I swallow hard, surprised that the words came bubbling out of me. "And despite my better judgment after everything that happened today, I still love you."

He moves fast, hurrying across the room to scoop me into his arms and hug me tight. I cling to him, reveling in the strength of his embrace.

"So when would you like to get married?"

I laugh. It's that or cry, and I've had enough tears to last me awhile. "We're not."

"Damn it, Nora—"

"We have a lot to talk about and work through before we

consider marriage. And frankly, you didn't propose. You didn't *ask*. You told. And I don't know if you've met me, but I'm not one to simply be led by the nose."

"Stubborn woman." But there's no heat in the words. He kisses the top of my head as his phone rings in his pocket. "That's Maggie's ringtone."

I step back as he answers the call.

"I'll be there soon. Thanks, Maggie."

"You have to go get Gabby," I guess.

"Yeah, Maggie has Bunko tonight."

"That woman has the best social life of anyone I know." I rub my hands together. I can't get warm.

"Come with me. We'll get takeout, and once Gabby goes to bed, we can continue this conversation."

Every bit of me longs to go with him.

"I'll pass."

"How long are you going to punish me?"

"I'm not." I reach for his hand, kiss the palm, and lay it on my heart. "I'm truly not trying to punish you."

"It feels like it from here."

"It's been a hell of a day, Carter." I take a deep breath and let it out slowly. "Emotional. I look like shit. I'd rather not answer all Gabby's questions, and trust me, she'll have questions if she sees me like this."

"I hadn't thought of that." He takes my hand and gives it a squeeze. "Are you okay, darling?"

"I will be. I just need a good night's sleep. I'll be good as new."

He kisses me, sliding those magical lips over mine, making my bones melt. Will there ever come a day when his kiss doesn't dissolve me into a puddle of need?

"If you need anything, just call. I can be here in ten minutes."

"I will."

"Oh, and I don't accept your resignation."

"I'm glad because I need the job." I smile ruefully. "Quitting was a rash decision."

"I need you," he says simply. "But you don't *need* the job, Nora."

"You'd better go before we have another fight. I'm not a kept woman just because—"

"Say it and I'll spank your ass."

I laugh as I push him to the door.

"Go away. I'll see you tomorrow."

"Good night." He kisses my forehead. "I love you."

Well, hell. I guess the tears are going to come after all.

"I love you, too."

"Why are you crying?"

"Hormones?"

His lips twitch and the dimple winks at me. "Get some rest."

I nod and shut the door behind him.

WELP, I'VE REACHED sloth status.

I've been on the couch for two hours, flipping channels and eating pizza I had delivered. I'm stuffed and moody.

I'm stoody.

I laugh at my own joke when my phone pings with a text from Gabby.

> **Gabby:** Hey. I heard dad tlk 2 gma, and he said ur mad.
> I hope I didn't do anything to screw everything up.

I smile. We need to talk about her grammar. Does it make me old to want to text properly? Probably.

> **Me:** You didn't do anything wrong, sweetie. Your dad
> and I just have some things to work out. It's all going
> to be okay.

I hope.

> **Gabby:** K. You should come over tonight.
> **Me:** Naw, I'm tired. I'll stay home for tonight, but I'm
> sure I'll see you tomorrow.
> **Gabby:** ☹
> **Me:** Don't pout. LOL Have a good night with your
> dad, and I'll see you soon. Be nice to him. I think he
> needs it.
> **Gabby:** K. Love you.
> **Me:** Love you more, kiddo.

My doorbell rings.

"Goodness, I'm popular today."

I'm surprised to see Sienna and London when I open the door. Their arms are full of bags.

"We brought food. And sparkling cider for you because you can't have wine. Sorry," London says as they walk past me to the kitchen. "But there's chocolate and cheesecake and french fries."

My eyes burn with fresh tears.

"Shit. You don't like cheesecake?" Sienna asks.

"I love cheesecake." I swipe at a tear and sit on a stool at the island. "This is just really unexpected."

"We wanted to come check on you," London says as she unloads bags, stows things in the fridge, and pours fries into bowls. "It's been a day for you."

"Understatement." I shove fries in my mouth, even though I'm already completely bursting at the seams. "There's pizza. I ordered some earlier."

"Nice," Sienna says. "Let's go sit in the living room. We'll pig out and talk about boys."

"A perfect evening." London winks and I lead the girls to the couch. Sienna sits across from us in my big overstuffed chair.

"I totally cross-examined Carter this afternoon after you left," she says as she pulls a slice of pepperoni pizza out of the box and bites the tip. "It was glorious. You should have been there."

"Tell me everything."

"He looked so miserable," she says and walks to the kitchen for paper towels. "But I was still brutal because he deserved it."

"I don't know much," London says. "I don't work there, and

I get everything secondhand from Finn, but even he doesn't say much. So start from the beginning and tell me everything."

So I do. I run through the last twenty-four hours, and Sienna fills in with her story of treating Carter like a criminal on the stand, which makes me laugh and feel emotional because I have these amazing women for friends.

I'm just a big cesspool of emotions today.

"What a jerk," London says, staring down at her fries. "I feel like I should march myself over to his place and smack him around a bit."

"He's been pummeled pretty good," I say with a shrug. "And then he told me we're getting married."

Silence. Sienna and London share a look of surprise, then turn their attention back to me.

"He *told* you?" London asks.

"Yep. Shoved a ring on my finger and said we'll be busy planning a wedding."

"This is why men die earlier than women," Sienna says matter-of-factly. "There's no ring on your finger now."

"Hell no, there isn't."

"I seriously love you," London says.

"I told him I wouldn't marry him out of convenience, that this isn't our parents' generation, and I can be an unwed mother."

"How did he take that?" Sienna asks.

"Not well. He was frustrated, and then I reminded him that he's never said he loves me."

"Wait." Sienna swallows her pizza. "He's *never* said it?"

"Nope." I shrug a shoulder. "But neither have I, to be fair. We established that we love each other. But no, I still didn't accept his nonproposal."

"Good," London says. "What's he thinking? He needs to do it right."

"He needs to actually *ask me*," I reply. "Not tell me."

"Cavemen," Sienna mutters. "They're all cavemen."

I lean back on the couch and moan. "You guys, I'm *so full*. I've eaten more food this evening than I eat in a week."

"We still have dessert," London says. "But we'll let this settle first."

"How are you feeling?" Sienna asks. "Do you *feel* pregnant?"

"Not really." I shrug and pat my normal-size belly. "I'm tired, but that's just because I had the day from hell. But it's really early. The doctor is thinking I'm less than six weeks along, which means I probably got pregnant the first time we had sex."

"Wow." Sienna's brows fly to her hairline. "Not only did the vasectomy not take, but Carter has Captain America sperm."

"Lucky him." I laugh and stand to gather empty bowls and the pizza box. "I still can't believe he asked me who the father is."

"I'd have castrated him, just for that alone," London says. "Then he wouldn't have to worry about getting anyone pregnant ever again."

"I was shocked. I told him to fuck himself."

"Good girl," Sienna says with a grin. "You do realize, even

though he hasn't asked you correctly, and you haven't accepted yet, you're our sister now, right? Like, you're ours forever."

"Forever and ever, amen," London agrees. "Whether you like it or not."

"I like it." We raise our glasses, and I clink my sparkling cider to their wine. "I like it a whole lot. I've never had sisters before."

"Are you an only child?"

"Yep."

"Well, I've had nothing but hard times with my brother, so being an only child isn't such a bad thing," London says.

"I love my sister, and she's doing better now with her new business and stuff, but yeah." Sienna nods her pretty head. "Having siblings is hard."

"I hope Gabby likes having a sibling." I frown. "I hope she takes the news well."

"She'll love it. That girl will smother a baby brother or sister with more love and attention than it knows what to do with," London replies.

We're quiet for a moment.

"You know, there are times I really want my mom." My voice is soft, and I swallow over the lump in my throat.

"Well, we can call her," Sienna says immediately. "We can bring her here anytime."

"No." I wipe a tear away. "You don't understand. My mom and I don't have a close relationship. I disappoint her. She doesn't agree with how I choose to live my life. Nothing I've ever done is good enough. She's cold and unaffectionate."

"Sounds like it's a good thing she didn't have more kids," Sienna mutters.

"You're right." I take a sip of cider and wish I could drink wine. "So I want the mom I *wish* she was. The nurturing, kind, loving mom I never had, you know?"

"I know you're not superclose yet, but Maggie is all those things," London says. "And if you ever need advice from a mother figure, I know she would be happy to listen."

"You're right." I nod and yawn. I'm just so sleepy. "I shudder to think what my mom will say when I tell her I'm expecting. She'll be disgusted. She'll rub it in my face that Richard will never take me back now that I have another man's seed growing in my womb."

"That's gross," Sienna says with a scowl.

"You don't want Rick the Dick anyway," London adds.

"Oh, trust me, I know. But it's not going to be a fun conversation. And it's not going to be any easier for Carter. His parents will be appalled that he's knocked up a girl from a small town in Ohio with no pedigree."

"They're all a bunch of assholes, and you don't need them," London insists. "You have a family, right here. And we love you both."

"Thank you."

"Let's put her to bed," Sienna says. "And then let her get some sleep. We all have work tomorrow."

"You're right," London says. "Come on with you."

"You do not have to put me to bed."

"Just think of us as stand-in moms tonight," Sienna says, taking my hand and leading me to the bedroom. I strip out of my clothes, unashamed of these ladies seeing me naked.

"Damn, I wish I had your boobs," London says with a sigh.

"And I want her hips," Sienna adds.

"And I want to be thin like the both of you." I laugh as I climb between the sheets. "We always want what we don't have."

"Well, I think we're all pretty fantastic, just as we are. Even if I don't have breasts," London says with a smile. She leans in to kiss my cheek. "Sleep well, friend."

"Good night," Sienna says. They shut off the light and leave, and I expect to lie awake, overthinking the events from the day. Normally, that's what I would have spent the evening alone doing.

And it occurs to me, as my eyes grow heavy, that my friends, my sisters, came over to distract me. To prevent me from doing exactly that.

Chapter Twenty

~Nora~

It's been three days since *the* day. The day I found out about the baby, and it all went to hell in a handbasket.

We've been working as usual. In fact, just about everything has gone back to normal, as if that day didn't even happen.

Well, almost everything.

It seems Carter's under the impression he can win my heart with copious amounts of flower deliveries. I'm talking movie-style flower deliveries. Every surface of my apartment is covered. My desk at work? Yep, covered.

And not just with white roses, although there are plenty of those, too. We're talking flowers of all colors and varieties.

My hunch is because the flower shops ran out of white roses.

It's Friday afternoon, and I've already received two deliveries this morning. It's getting to be ridiculous.

"Hi."

I look up, over the wall of posies, to see the delivery kid standing at my desk once again.

"More?"

He nods. "And I'm scheduled to come back in a couple of hours."

"No." I shake my head, surprising the poor young guy. "It's not that I don't appreciate your work, but this is silly. I don't have any more space for flowers."

"I don't know what to tell you, lady, it's my job to deliver them." He passes me the bouquet, shrugs, and whistles as he saunters to the elevator.

Enough.

I stand and carry the bouquet into Carter's office. He's on a call, and his brows raise in surprise when he sees me, so he cuts the call short and hangs up.

"You shouldn't have, darling." His lips twitch in humor.

"I didn't." I set the flowers on his desk. "Carter, you have to stop with the flowers. I don't have any more space for them. My house looks like a botanical garden, and my desk is so full of flowers, I don't have any space for actual *work*. You have to stop."

"No." His eyes shine with love as he watches me. I realize now he's been looking at me like this for weeks, I was just too blind, or stubborn, to realize it was love and not just affection. "I don't have to stop anything. It pleases me to send you flowers."

"Then they're going to live in your office because I'm fresh out of room."

He catches my hand in his before I can march out of the office and pulls me into his lap. He kisses me softly, cupping my cheek.

"I don't have time for your shenanigans."

"Sure you do." He kisses me again. "I'm the boss, and I just put it on your schedule."

"You think you're the boss, but *I* make the schedules around here."

"So sassy," he murmurs. "Are we still on for this evening?"

"Yes." We're going out to dinner, our first date since our big fight, and I'm more than ready for it.

"Well, add this to our schedule; we're leaving at two this afternoon." I frown, but before I can say anything, he says, "That's not a request, darling."

"Yes, sir." I give him a mock salute and kiss him firmly before wiggling out of his lap. "If I'm leaving early, I'd better get back to my desk. I have lots to do."

"Be sure to eat a banana," he calls after me.

He's constantly feeding me. Asking me if I'm hungry, if I feel okay.

I have a feeling he's going to dote on me during this entire pregnancy, and frankly, it feels pretty damn good.

"SO WE CAME all the way to Florida for dinner?" I ask, standing in the condo at the beach, staring at Carter in confusion. We left work at two and drove straight to the airport, where we took the company plane to Jacksonville, and then Carter drove me to a quiet restaurant, where we enjoyed a delicious Italian dinner.

And now we're back at the condo. I'm not complaining. In fact, I've discovered I love being at the ocean more than just about anywhere else.

But this is elaborate for a simple date.

"I thought we could use a weekend away," he says. "Why don't we go for a walk on the beach? It's a lovely night for it."

He's different tonight. I can't put my finger on it, but something is just . . . different. He looks so at ease, so calm compared to how he's been for the past couple of weeks.

Maybe it's the beach that has this effect on both of us.

"Sure."

We walk, hand in hand, to the bridge that crosses over the dunes, and down to the sand, where we kick off our flip-flops and leave them by the bridge. We'll retrieve them on our way back.

The sand is coarse, but it feels good on my feet. We make our way down to the wet sand, which is easier to walk on, and walk south. The sun is just starting to set, shooting orange and purple through the sky.

Carter's right, it's a lovely evening for a walk on the beach.

We're quiet, listening to the waves and wind.

"Look at those birds." I point to little white birds with long beaks, poking holes in the sand.

"They're eating little insects in the sand," he says with a smile. "Watching the pelicans dive into the water is even better."

"Oh, I want to see that."

He smiles down at me and leads me farther down the beach, to the driftwood log I found him on the last time we were here.

"Let's take a rest."

"This is the perfect spot." I sit and take a deep breath of salty air. The breeze is in my hair, and I never want to leave this place. "I love it here."

"I know." He clears his throat and puts his hand in his pocket.

Holy shit. This is it. He's going to propose.

But rather than pull out a ring, he has a letter.

"This is something Gabby wanted me to give you." He offers me the envelope, and as I rip it open, he leans forward, his elbows on his knees, and watches the water.

The letter is written in Gabby's handwriting. I can tell she took her time to make it as pretty as she could. The paper is pink, and she's dotted her *i*'s with hearts.

I smile. She's so funny.

Dear Nora,

Dad invited me to come with you to the beach, but I decided to stay in NY with Grandma. I can always go down there another time, and you're just going to be mushy and kiss and stuff. You know, gross stuff. But I hope you have a lot of fun this weekend.

Dad told me that I'm going to be a big sister, and

I can't wait! I promise, I'll help with everything. You won't have to do everything by yourself. I mean, I don't love the idea of changing poopy diapers, but if I have to, I will. Having a sister is going to be awesome.

I know I haven't been easy, and I'm sorry. I'm so sorry, Nora. Grandma said that sometimes we hurt the people we love the most, and I guess I was just acting out, trying to hurt you as much as I was hurting. Because I love you so much. Even before you and Dad got together, you've been there for me. I love spending time with you and helping you decorate your apartment. I hope we still do those things.

I never really thought about my dad falling in love. It's weird. But if he's going to be with someone, I'm so glad he's with you. Because you're the best! You make us laugh and you make my dad really, really happy. So thanks for that.

You're the best friend I've ever had.

And now, Dad's gonna ask you a really (really is underlined four times) *important question, okay?*

Love,
Gabrielle Shaw

I fold the letter and tuck it away, and when I look up, Carter is kneeling on one knee before me.

"Oh my God."

He grins, that dimple that I love so much deep in his left cheek, and reaches for my hand.

"I did this wrong before, and I apologize for that," he begins. I bite my lip, listening intently to every single word. I want to sear this moment into my brain. "I've wanted to propose to you for weeks. I've carried a ring in my pocket, waiting for the perfect time.

"But that moment didn't come, and now I know why. And no, I'm not ready now because we're having a baby, or because I feel obligated to link our lives together. Obligation isn't a part of this at all, Nora, and I want to make that clear."

"I understand."

He licks his lips, and for just a moment, I see a flash of nervousness in his ocean-blue eyes.

"I also realize why it was hard for me to put into words how much I love you. I've never loved anyone else the way I do you, Nora. You will never know a day when you're unloved by me, because your soul is so tangled in mine, there will never be a time that I'd let you go.

"There's a magic in what we have together. You've been a constant in my life for so long, and yet, falling in love with you was so easy, I could have done so with my eyes closed. I laugh harder with you. I *feel* more with you. And at the end of the day, whenever I hear a joke or need to share something, it's *you* I want to share it with.

"I trust you with my daughter, with her heart. And she looks at you like you've hung the moon, even when she's angry. And, unfortunately, there will be plenty of angry moments, but there will be happy ones, too.

"I want you next to me during all of it. As my partner. As my best friend. As my wife."

He leans in and presses a sweet kiss to my cheek.

"Will you please marry me, Nora?"

"Oh yes." He slips the ring on my finger, and I frown. "This isn't the same ring you had the other day."

"That ring was cursed," he says with a laugh. "And you'd already seen it. This moment called for something fresh and new."

I wrap my arms around his shoulders and he spins me in a circle, right here on the beach as the sun slides into the water.

"I love you so much," I say before I kiss his neck.

"I love you," he says. "And now, I'm going to take my fiancée back to our condo, so I can make love to her all damn night."

"That's the best idea you've ever had."

MORNINGS AT THE beach are my favorite.

Oh, who am I kidding? Everything at the beach is my favorite.

But this morning, I'm sitting on the balcony, sipping decaf coffee and watching the water.

Last night was unexpected.

I stare down at the huge rock on my finger as it sparkles in the sunshine.

I figured Carter would propose eventually, but he went above and beyond any of my expectations. And then we came back here and he made good on his word, making love to me until the sun came up.

So it was a slow morning.

I pulled on a swimsuit cover-up rather than a robe. It's too warm for terry cloth. But the blue cotton is light and covers me perfectly.

The glass door slides open, and Carter steps out with a tray. He sets it on the table next to me, then leans in to kiss me on the cheek.

"I brought fruit and a few pastries. I'm going for a run on the beach."

I see an envelope on the tray as well and frown up at him.

"You can stay."

"No, this doesn't concern me." He kisses me deeply and then pulls away. "I'll take that run and give you some space."

He kisses my hand, presses it to his heart, then returns inside the condo, leaving me alone.

I reach for a strawberry, not in a hurry to tear open the letter.

When I've eaten half the food on the tray and finished my coffee, I watch as Carter runs down the beach, headed toward our driftwood.

In tidy handwriting on the envelope, it reads, *To Her.*

I carefully open the sealed envelope and pull out a letter from Darcy.

Hello,

I hope you're having a delicious glass of wine, and maybe some dessert as you read this. I want you to think of this letter as girl talk between friends, even though I'm the only one talking.

So you're the one Carter has chosen to spend the rest of his life with. I don't have to tell you that you're a lucky woman. You already know that. But I'd like to tell you that he's lucky, too. Because if he chose you, you're an incredible person. A woman capable of loving not only Carter but also our Gabby girl, and not every woman is up for the challenge of raising a child that didn't come from her body.

It feels condescending to try to give you advice. I don't mean it that way. But I know this man well, and there are some bits and pieces I can share.

When he's afraid, he'll clam up. You'll think he's mad or that he's pulling away from you, but he really just shuts down when he's scared. It pisses me off, and I try to be patient with him.

I hope you have better luck with that than I have.

He hates peanut butter. I don't know why. But trust me, it's a thing.

My family will yank you into their fold and love you. That's just who they are. My parents are solid and they

*love their kids fiercely. I admit, I'm more of a daddy's
girl. You'll absolutely love him.*

I have to pause and wipe a tear. Darcy's father passed away
not even a year after she did. But she's right, I did like him very
much.

*Gabby's just a little girl. I'm sure you can imagine
how much it's killing me to leave her. She still needs
me. But it's reassuring to know that you're there for
her. For all the moments that I'll miss. Her graduation, college years, her wedding, and even having her
own babies.*

*I really was looking forward to being covered in
grandchildren.*

*Do that for me, won't you? Love her, and her babies,
the way I would.*

*It won't be easy. None of it. But it'll be so worth it.
And even though you don't need it, you have my blessing.*

Congratulations.

*Love,
Darcy*

Well. What's a girl supposed to say to that?
I read it once again before setting it aside and settling back

in my chair. I liked Darcy. I didn't know her well, but the few times I had any interaction with her, I liked her very much.

My phone pings with a text from Gabby.

Gabby: YOU SAID YES!! Show me the rock.

I laugh and take a picture of my left hand, then send it through.

Me: Your dad didn't show you?

Gabby: No, I didn't see him after he picked it up. Wow, it's so pretty! Do you like it?

Me: What's not to love.

Gabby: Right? So pretty. Yay! Also, I don't want to make this weird, but I'm gonna call you Mom, unless you hate the idea. Because I called Darcy Mommy. I was still little then. And you're my mom. Okay?

I pause to take a breath. It seems the Shaw women are trying to turn me into a giant puddle of mushy goo today.

Me: Totally okay.

Gabby: Cool. Okay, Grandma's taking me to the movies. Love you, Mom!

Me: Love you more, kiddo.

I set my phone aside and watch as Carter jogs toward me, his run almost finished. I pinch my arm, and then frown at the sting.

Yep, I'm awake.

And this life, this beautiful amazing life full of new sisters, a big family, a daughter that makes me crazy, and the sexiest man on earth, is mine.

It seems I believe in happy endings after all.

Epilogue

~Maggie~

Five years later . . .

Is she okay?" Nora asks. We're sitting on the porch of my little guesthouse on the family property in Martha's Vineyard, watching as all the children play in the pool.

"Oh yes, dear. This little love is just snoozing the afternoon away." I feel her little round cheek and smile when her lips pucker. "Eliza is such a pretty name."

"Thank you," Nora replies with a soft smile, watching her youngest daughter sleep in my arms. "She's a good baby."

"You were due for one," I say as I look out over the yard, searching for our little four-year-old. "Lucy was a handful when she was an infant."

"She's still a handful," Nora agrees and then scoots to the edge of her chair when she sees Lucy stepping a little too close to the edge of the deep end of the pool. "Oh, baby, don't get so close."

"There's Gabby, swooping in to get her," I say. Gabby's seventeen and completely in love with her little sisters. "Oh, look at that. Lucy just tossed her hair and cocked her hip the way Gabby does."

"She's mimicking *everything* Gabby does. She insists she needs a phone, so she can text like Gabby."

"A handful for certain," I say with a soft laugh. "She'll keep us all on our toes."

"I'm not ready for Gabby to be a senior in high school." Nora's voice is wistful. "She grew up too fast."

"Children have a habit of doing that to us."

Finn, Quinn, and Carter are in the water, helping all the babies swim, keeping an eye on everyone.

Quinn and Sienna's little boy, Charlie, is three and not afraid of the water in the least.

He's exactly like his father, that one.

And London and Finn's boy, Harrison, is just a few months younger than Charlie, so they like to get into trouble together.

Yes, this brood of mine will keep me busy for years to come, and I'm happy for it.

"I can't believe this is my first time here," Nora says. "I guess we always just go down to Florida, but this is lovely, too."

"Oh yes. So Finn owned the house to the left, and London's family owned the house on the right. This small guesthouse, where we're sitting, is new. Rather than sell one of the properties, Finn and London decided to have the property lines changed, so it's one big property. They had the trees and fence removed between them, built this little house for me, or other guests, and now it's just one big space for us to use. It took two years to finish it all, so this is the first summer for family vacations to Martha's Vineyard. I hope we come every summer."

"So it's a compound," Nora says in surprise. She slips on her sunglasses and sits back in her chair. "I feel like a Kennedy."

"I suppose *compound* is the right word for it." I shift the baby to my shoulder and lightly tap her little back. "Go out there and play with them," I urge my sweet daughter-in-law. "Or go sit with Sienna and London and relax."

"Are you sure?"

"Eliza and I are happy as clams. I'll come find you when she's hungry."

"Well, then I won't turn it down." She stands but rather than leave the porch, she leans in to kiss my cheek. "Thank you, Maggie. I sure do love you."

"I love you, too, dear."

She smiles and walks off the porch. She exchanges words with Carter, who winks at his wife, and then she's off with the other moms.

If you'd have asked me when I was young how I pictured living out my golden years, this would have been close to what my answer would be.

Surrounded by my family. Covered in grandchildren.

But I would have had my darling husband by my side, and my daughter would be healthy and whole.

I miss them both deeply. I long for them.

But if things hadn't happened the way they did, I wouldn't have this sweet babe in my arms, or Nora, the daughter of my heart.

My boys chose wisely when it came to their girls. They're wonderful parents, smart women, and they keep my boys on their toes.

As it should be.

About the Author

KRISTEN PROBY has published more than forty titles, many of which have hit the *USA Today*, *New York Times*, and *Wall Street Journal* bestseller lists. She continues to self-publish, best known for her With Me in Seattle and Boudreaux series, and is also proud to work with William Morrow, a division of Harper-Collins, with the Fusion and Romancing Manhattan series.

Kristen and her husband, John, make their home in her hometown of Whitefish, Montana, with their two cats.

BOOKS BY **KRISTEN PROBY**

LISTEN TO ME
A Fusion Novel; Book One

Five best friends open a hot new restaurant, but one of them gets much more than she bargained for when a sexy former rock star walks through the doors-and into her heart.

CLOSE TO YOU
A Fusion Novel; Book Two

Since the day she met Landon Palazzo, Camilla LaRue, part owner of the wildly popular restaurant Seduction, has been head-over-heels in love. And when Landon joined the Navy right after high school, Cami thought her heart would never recover. Now, Landon is back and he looks better than ever.

BLUSH FOR ME
A Fusion Novel; Book Three

When Kat, the fearless, no-nonsense bar manager of Seduction, and Mac, a successful but stubborn business owner, find themselves unable to play nice or even keep their hands off each other, it'll take some fine wine and even hotter chemistry for them to admit they just might be falling in love.

THE BEAUTY OF US
A Fusion Novel; Book Four

Riley Gibson is over the moon at the prospect of having her restaurant, Seduction, on the Best Bites TV network. This could be the big break she's been waiting for. But the idea of having an in-house show on a regular basis is a whole other matter. And when she meets Trevor Cooper, the show's executive producer, she's stunned by their intense chemistry.

SAVOR YOU
A Fusion Novel; Book Five

Cooking isn't what Mia Palazzo does, it's who she is. She's built a stellar menu for her restaurant, Seduction. Now, after being open for only a few short years, Mia's restaurant is being featured on Best Bites TV. Then Camden Sawyer, the biggest mistake of her life, walks into her kitchen... As Mia and Camden face off, neither realizes how high the stakes are as their reputations are put on the line and their hearts are put to the ultimate test.

ALL THE WAY
Romancing Manhattan, Book One

Three brothers get more than they bargain for as they practice law, balance life, and navigate love in and around New York City.

ALL IT TAKES
Romancing Manhattan, Book Two

In Kristen Proby's second novel in her Romancing Manhattan series, a playboy vows never to commit—until he meets the one woman he's tempted to break his promise for.

AFTER ALL
Romancing Manhattan, Book Three

The last sizzling novel in Kristen Proby's Romancing Manhattan series finds a widower falling deeply in love again with a woman who has scars of her own.